Aliki Roussin is a poet, artist and photographer. She divides her time between Spetses and Athens in Greece and London, where live her two adult daughters. She has illustrated this book with photographs of painted sea pebbles that 'glance at us rounded, solid and pure in deathless light'.

BENEATH IDLE GODS

by

Aliki Roussin

with illustrations by the author

with thanks to
Maria Powell & Parina Douzina

ISBN 0-936315-51-2
STARHAVEN, 42 Frognal, London NW3 6AG
books@starhaven.org.uk
https://starhavenpress.wordpress.com/
https://www.facebook.com/starhaven.org.uk/

Typeset in Palatino Linotype

For Melissa & Natalia

I.

For weeks on end snow had whitened the world. Screeching winds now rose up, rupturing its blanketing silence. Mount Olympus, the gods' abode, resounded with eerie murmurs. The world below for the first time was invisible and so were its people. The immortal Olympians, concerned about the planet's fate and its inhabitants after centuries of inaction, sent Hermes the messenger to find out what was happening.

Hermes tied on his winged sandals, put on his invisible cloak and took off, wondering where to start. The snakes entwined into one on his shaft, wishing to help him, hissed that a visit to Paradise might be a good start. It was a place they also knew well.

Holding a cup of freshly brewed Arabica as black as the devil's sweat, Merena looked at the snow on the apple trees in her garden. It reminded her of a fairy landscape where she had once experienced a wondrous Odyssey. Taking a sip, she closed her eyes. Time bent and buckled, and a journey unfolded that had begun in another garden in the eastern part of a province called Eden.

It was a day like all the rest in Paradise. Early morning sun absorbed the last drops of moisture on the leaves, and birds in a frantic chorus greeted the day. Eve opened her eyes and, yawning, looked at Adam lying fast asleep next to her. His mouth, half-opened, was puffing out air followed by a slight groan. Stretching out her hand, she caressed his ribs. Adam grunted and turned on his side.

'He must have had a late night watching the stars again,' mumbled Eve. 'It's no good trying to wake him. I might as well go and collect some food.'

Eve had a strange feeling as she started off, but did not know what it was. For a long time she had been wondering about things but when she tried to communicate them to Adam, he was not forthcoming. When she asked him how he knew she was created from his rib since he had been asleep when it happened, he replied that she should not query the heavens. And when a lion came by and Adam ordered it to sit, Eve, sensing that the animal wanted to continue to roam, asked Adam why he had commanded it to do as he said.

'Because God said that I could have dominion over the whole earth and all its creatures,' was Adam's reply. Eve again had felt uncomfortable but did not know quite why. Now as she went off, she was wondering what happened when Adam slept. He did not wake up when she touched him. He did not see her hand on his forehead. What happened to her when she was asleep? Did Adam touch her?

How could she see him with her eyes shut?

Caressing a wild cat that happened into her path, Eve stopped to collect some ripe pomegranates – this is how Adam had named them – when she heard a voice.

'Good morning, Eve,' said the snake, the most subtle of all the other beasts God had created.

'How do you know my name?'

'I know your name and I also know that you care for living things.'

'What does care mean?'

'It means to love, protect, and look after them.'

'I do not know these words but I feel what you say. Where did you learn them? From God?'

'Not necessarily. It has to do with the duality of my nature. I store in my body powerful venom. It can kill and at the same time it can cure. It depends on the circumstances how it is going to be used. It is the knowledge of this duality that gives me lucidity about life.'

Eve was taken aback. Adam never spoke to her that way. He never told her about venom, duality and lucidity.

'Who are you then?' asked Eve.

'I am the snake.'

'Well, snake, I feel good because there is another one in Paradise who can talk even though your talk is not like Adam's or mine. Yet I feel what you say. I was on my way to the river to get some water, so come along.'

Soon enough they reached the river. Its waters were reflecting the sun rays and the flowers of the earth. Picking up a discarded shell of a coconut, Eve bent over to collect water, but what she saw made her fall back yelling.

'What is the matter, Eve? Why are you yelling?'

'There is someone looking at me in the water. God said he only created Adam and me and now there is someone else.'

The snake looked at the water and saw Eve's reflection.

'That person in the water is you.'

'Me?'

'It is your reflection; it will do whatever you do. Let me come near you and look into the water again. You see? Now I am next to you in the water.'

Eve was lost for words. She looked at the snake, then at its reflection, then back at her own reflection. Stretching her hand out, she tried to touch her image but it all disappeared, leaving ripples on the water.

'We are gone,' Eve cried and for the first time she felt something strange because she wanted her image to return.

The snake, understanding her longing, told her to keep still and the image would reappear – as indeed happened.

Eve looked again and again at her reflection. She wanted to touch it but dared not, because she knew it would vanish.

'Put your hand on your heart,' said the snake.

Eve did so and so did the Eve of the river.

'Lift your hair and hold it on top of your head.'

Eve did so and so did the crowned Eve of the river.

'Tell her something.'

Eve said, 'Good morning' and the silent Eve of the water moved her lips.

'She did not reply,' said Eve.

'This is because you are having a monologue. People reply back when you have a dialogue like the two of us and, if Adam joins in, then things will be different again.'

'Why?'

'Because then you are aware of someone else's presence – my presence – and you cannot be exactly as you are.'

'How can I be and not be?'

'This is called questioning and questioning leads to a lot of trouble. It can lead to some knowledge and some understanding, but not too much and not by all.'

Eve had heard this word 'knowledge' from God. There was a tree called 'the tree of life' and a tree called 'the tree of knowledge', which they were not allowed to feed from. This snake seems to know about knowledge, she thought. Is it because of its poisonous duality, or had it tasted the forbidden fruit? It was too much for Eve. Suddenly all she wanted was to be with Adam. Picking up her fruits and water, she thanked the snake for telling her about her reflection and said she had to go, because Adam was waiting for his food.

'I understand,' said the snake, 'this is what caring is about. When shall I see you again then? Tomorrow?'

'Perhaps,' replied Eve, her eyes glued to the ground.

'This is an interesting word, "perhaps". Where did you hear it?'

'I made it up.'

'Well, then, perhaps I will see you tomorrow. This was a good day and a good start.'

Eve did not want to ask any more questions or what 'a good start' meant. The snake made her feel uncomfortable in one way but in another way made her sense that there was something else in Paradise. Only what?

'Where on Paradise have you been?' Adam shouted as he saw Eve appearing through the bushes.

'I had a day not like the rest,' Eve replied, unperturbed, handing him the fruits and water. 'I saw my reflection, had a monologue, then a dialogue like we have now, and a snake told me about duality and that I care for all living things.'

'Eve, in God's name, what is all this? What are these words, and who is this snake?'

'It is not like us, but it could be like us. I don't know exactly how to say it. It seems to have some knowledge.'

Adam was restless. How can this snake have knowledge,

and why did it make Eve's eyes glare? What was a reflection? Or a duality? He had to go and find out and most importantly dominate the dangerous creature.

'Eve stay here and clean the fallen leaves from the ground while I go and find that snake.'

'No, I won't. I am not sweeping the leaves.'

'What?' said Adam, feeling blood rushing to his temples for the first time. 'God said that you must obey me.'

'I am coming with you because I know where the snake is. God will find nothing wrong in my wanting to be with you. This is the reason he created me after all.'

Adam could not understand what was going on. Everything had been so calm up until then, but it was not the same now. He suddenly felt alone, even though Eve was there. He wanted to speak to God and be told by Him that all was well, but He was nowhere to be found. Without saying a word, his heart beating much faster, Adam followed Eve.

They both walked in silence, and it was not long before they met the snake.

'Good morning again,' said the snake. 'Perhaps is a short time,' it added with a wink.

'What kind of a beast are you and what are these strange words and things you are showing to Eve?' asked Adam, the blood rushing to his head again. 'I command you to stop all this and get out of our way.'

'Aha!' came the snake's reply. 'Dear Adam, it is you who came looking for me and, please, allow me to inform you that it is not so easy to command me. I have a free will and can chose for myself what I do and what I don't.'

Adam felt like bashing this animal, and the sensation was new to him. First Eve had been disobedient, and now this beast was doing exactly the same. As if this was not enough, Eve kept staring at the snake with an expression on her face he had only seen once – when she woke up and saw him for the first time. But before Adam had time to act, Eve asked:

'What is a free will?'

'It means I can be the master of my own life. Of course this is not easy. It requires a lot of thought and also the knowledge that I am responsible for my actions, making life at times a burden. But if we are free and responsible, there is no master. We can take our lives into our own hands.'

Adam could not believe his ears. How could life be a burden and how could he be his own responsible master when the only master was his God? For Adam every day was the same, and God provided. Why should he listen to this beast? All he wanted was to take Eve and go, but he had to reply in order to show that he was in control.

'God said that we are free to live here and have everything. Life in Paradise is so good, why should one disobey him? I've had enough of this. I command you, snake, according to God's will not to come near Eve again or be seen around.'

Dragging Eve by the hand he started walking away, but the snake continued:

'How can you be free when you are forbidden to taste the fruits of knowledge and of life? Especially when someone commands you to do so. Perhaps God created this situation to give you a choice. It is limited in a sense, but it is still a choice. You can keep going as you are or decide to try something different.'

'Different?' said Adam, stalling.

'Yes, yes,' said Eve. 'I sense this. It is like when I go out to pick up food. There are many different fruits. Some days I pick from one tree, other days from another.'

'I feel I should listen only to God,' Adam said. 'After all, he created me after his own image. I am like him.'

'Adam,' continued the snake persuasively, 'God is a solitary figure. He created all this, and now it is done. A hunky-dory paradise and you two the most important of all his creatures, eating the same boring fruits every day.'

'I am pleased you can see that we are most important,' Adam interrupted.

'Not because you are the centre of the universe,' continued the snake unperturbed, 'but because you could bring about changes, bad ones and good. And by doing so, you could make His existence worthwhile. The greatest gift He gave you was Eve, so you are not alone. Of course He never experienced companionship, so the combination might turn out not to be perfect in the long run. But He did the best He could under the circumstances. He also created me to help awaken your consciousness. I am the middleman in a way, and it is not an envious position to be in. For whatever happens to you, I too will have to bear the consequences.'

'What is consciousness?' Eve asked.

'To be able to turn inside-out in a manner of speaking. Everything begins with Consciousness, and nothing is worth anything except through it. To try and understand who you are. One will never get it right – it is a bit like trying to catch running water – but the closer you get, the closer you are in understanding your solitary God and acting in a way that might help others. You won't necessarily be understood by them, or even appreciated, but you will be closer to yourself, which is the image of God. I am aware you might not understand what I am saying because you need to experience it.'

'What is experience?' asked Adam.

'To live. I cannot explain because it is personal. You have to live it for yourself. It is different for everyone.'

'But are we not living now?' Eve interrupted.

'In order to live, you must know that you have to die. To leave your body behind because your time on earth is lim-

ited, like everything else. Life, death and time are bound together, like Adam and you. Time carries us but there comes
a moment when we have to carry it. This is the future, and it
is in the future that you will find out what I am trying to say.
It is difficult to explain life and death to you because they
are inseparable. Even though you are together, you will discover that one's life can be shared but not lived by another;
the same goes for death. I can see on your faces now that I've
said too much and, perhaps, I should let you go. If, however,
you wish to see me again, I'll be here tonight.'

'Let us go?' Adam replied. 'It is not up to you to hold us
here. We are free to come and go and you seem to forget that
you are still under my dominion.'

'As you wish,' answered the snake with a wink, slowly
disappearing among the thick foliage.

Adam and Eve walked away like two fateful shadows
clinging to earth. The seed of a schism was apparent, however microscopic.

'Let's go to the river,' said Eve, dragging Adam along. 'I
want to see your reflection.'

Reaching the bank, they sat quietly side by side, their figures mirrored in the crystalline waters. Adam looked at his
reflection, then Eve's.

'You don't look like me,' he said.

'I know.'

'You know?'

'Yes, I am beginning to know myself. I seem to be the
space between what I want to be and what others made me
to be. Like the space between myself and the reflection.'

'Do you think you are different because you came from my
rib? Did you come from my rib?'

'I don't know. Does it matter?'

'You don't know? Then only God knows.'

'Perhaps, what I know is that you don't like the snake. It is because it is different. One does not necessarily have to like it, but I can feel its words. I know you like Paradise, the earth, the animals, and so do I. I have walked from one side to the other and seen what there is to be seen. Picked up every single fruit and tasted it, played with and caressed the animals, but there is something else I am looking for. I don't know what it is. Perhaps it is not here or, if it is, I will never find it, because I need to experience something different. I know that you too are seeking the same thing. I watch you sometimes gazing at the distant stars. You wonder what they are, if they could be reached. The difference between you and me is a matter of distance, not essence.'

'Essence? Where did you find this word?'

'It came after we looked at our reflections. It means the core of things, what really matters. I want to taste the forbidden fruits. I know there is no coming back. God might be displeased, but perhaps this is not a bad thing. He forbids us to taste them because He wants to protect us. After all, there has never been a dialogue between the two of you. It was more of a monologue. He talked and you agreed. We will never find out His intentions. He might not know either. As the snake said: 'He did everything on his own.' This is the difference between Him and us. We can be together, near each other, seeking knowledge, live and die, or you can be like God on your own in Paradise. What do you want? to stare at the stars, or get closer to them?'

Adam was lost for words. He felt for his God, but something had changed. He did not see Him anymore as a powerful master, but more like him. He suddenly understood what the snake meant by the burden of life. Yet to try and get this knowledge of life seemed very difficult. Part of him wanted to put all this behind and go on as if the snake had never appeared, but another part of him wanted to try the unknown. Had he been on his own he might have stuck with Paradise. Eve, however, wanted something else and was prepared to try it. Perhaps this was the duality the snake had spoken about. Adam had no option but to take a leap into the unknown.

'I want us to be together,' he said.

'So do I.'

'But before we eat the fruits, we must see the snake once more, because there is something I need to ask.'

'What is it?'

'It is about the trees.'

The snake was waiting for them. It knew this would be the last time they would see each other in Paradise.

'One day can change everything,' it thought.

Before long, Adam and Eve appeared. Eve spoke:

'We want to try the forbidden fruits because we want to know about life and death. Is this bad or good? You must know because, as you said, your venom can kill and cure.'

'Seeking what is true is not seeking what is desirable, and there is no true creation without a secret. Neither does bad or good exist until you create it through your actions,' replied the snake. 'This is all I can say. The rest you must find out for yourselves.'

Glancing at them longer than normal, he slowly disappeared among the thick foliage and the deafening singing of the birds of Paradise.

Adam looked at Eve. All of a sudden he understood what beauty was. Taking her hand softly, they went to the trees. Adam cut an apple and offered it to Eve. Eve cut another apple and offered it to Adam.

Merena's coffee was finished. She stared at the bottom of the cup. It was clean. In the older days when freeze-dried coffee was not so much in, she used to drink the thick black stuff which left a crust at the bottom, out of which women could read the future. In this case, however, it was obvious what happened next. Adam and Eve were chased out of eternity's springboard, but not because they had sinned.

They could not visualise what was in store for them and therefore remained innocent.

Their first child, Hope, was born in exile. Hope showed them how to laugh and to work hard, because everything that makes humans work utilises hope. Their second child, Love, made them shed their first tears of pain. Even though she was elusive, she never left them, lingering by their side until their dying day. Their third child was named Eternity, because it made them discover all the truths their hands could touch and create works of art.

Adam called Eve 'Mother of all living things' and Eve called Adam 'the apple of her eye.' Together and apart they learned to think, creating a conscious world where noble and criminal deeds occurred.

The snake too had its downfall. It was condemned to drag its body on its belly on the dusty earth, but it also had its compensations because it was able to shed its skin and be transformed. Furthermore, it remained the symbol of healing power on Asclepius' shaft and peace on Hermes' caduceus. As for God's story, it was reinvented and reinterpreted ad infinitum. Sometimes the people's master was a god of darkness; at other times many anthropomorphic gods ruled. In most cases, however, the prevailing God was light shining upon the mortal faces of men and women and vice versa.

Taking a bite from a ripe apple, Merena gazed at the splendid scenery stretching outside her window. Snow had covered all the trees in the garden, spreading like a white linen sheet, similar to the one her mother Eve had given her when she got married. Perhaps this world she lived in had stopped reflecting in a higher universe. Yet its heavenly forms were stored in the host images of this earth, right here, beyond her window. And a single truth, if obvious, was enough to guide an existence through the intricate paths of this wondrous life.

Lighting a cigarette, she wondered: Did it ever snow in Paradise?

II.

We have been idle for centuries on Olympus, thought Hermes. The human race seems to be in a teleporting era, but throughout time they seem to like apples. I am surprised, though, that they still know about my caduceus. I wonder if people can be beamed up in the skies. Perhaps I should ask Asclepius who is roaming among the stars to help me. I hope Zeus won't mind, and I won't be cast out in the cosmic chaos like he was.

Having wandered among the stars for aeons, Asclepius was able to inform Hermes that things were indeed very different. Rubbish was circulating round the blue planet where Mount Olympus was located, and people were traveling in strange metallic devices. Some were even staying in space for long periods. He remembered a human who was in despair while travelling in space because her only companion – a dog – was dying. Asclepius tried to revive the beast but it was too late. Taking pity on the heartbroken traveller, he remained around until she returned to earth. He repeated her story now to Hermes as she had recounted it to him.

'I remember during the early years of my life always being surrounded by my family. They were all beautiful, tall, blue-eyed people. At the time I thought that if I cried a lot my dark eyes would fade to blue and I too, would become beautiful. To my surprise they never did, but the search for beauty started during those early years with three stories.

'I was very young when my mother read me the first one. It was a big beautifully-coloured book called "The Ugly Duckling". To this day I don't know why she made this choice. Was it, I often wondered, the doctor's kind comment at my birth, "She will turn into a swan"? Whatever my mother's reason, the outcome turned out beneficial. Besotted with the tale, I made her read it over and over until I knew it by heart. I therefore owe my passion for reading to "The Ugly Duckling". Ducks also made me realise something else later: though they appear to glide effortlessly, their struggle is hidden underneath the water, invisible to the naked eye.

'It was my mother again who told me the second story a few years after that, when I asked her to define beauty. She replied with a tale from The Bible. This surprised me, as she was an agnostic and more in tune with Socrates' philosophy than Christianity. Not a very common characteristic for a Greek woman at that time. The story went like this:

'One day Christ and his disciples were taking a walk when a terrible stench reached their nostrils. They pulled their clothes up to cover their faces while trying to locate the source of the appalling smell of decay. It was not long before when they saw the cadaver of a dog. They grimaced and said how horrible it looked, how unbearable the smell was. Christ, completely calm and unperturbed, turned around and said: "Did you notice how beautiful his teeth were?"

'I felt what the story meant deeply and, as I grew up, I realised that something inhuman lay at the heart of all beauty – like the primitive hostility of a contradictory world rising to face one across millennia. I tried hard to discover a balance within this permanent contradiction surrounding us. I knew that somewhere, amidst the odd vegetation of a wasteland, I could glimpse both beauty and the beast. But I was still too young and had not yet acquired the necessary tenacity to do so, so instead all I did was rebel.

'The third story took place in another dimension, but the after-effects still resonate. I could even go as far as to say that at that crucial point in my life, reality, history and myth fused into a metaphysical experience.

'It was November 3 in 1957, when history changed. The Soviet Union successfully launched Sputnik2 into space with a live dog onboard, Laika. As a technological achievement, Sputnik (travelling companion) caught the world's attention and the American public off-guard. They feared that the Soviet Union's ability to launch satellites translated into a capability of launching ballistic missiles that could carry nuclear weapons. I remember that at the time I was more worried about the dog than the grownups' concern about the threat of nuclear weapons. Gazing at the sky night after night, I hoped to catch a glimpse of Laika's face looking through the window. To my disappointment I only saw it in photographs. I have kept these photographs all these years and, as I look at them now, yellow and creased by time, I recall my journey with Laika, which has yet to end.

'She was a three year old female part-Samoyed terrier mongrel recruited from the streets of Moscow. Named Kudryavka (Little Curly) by her trainers, she was officially renamed Laika (Barker) after her breed. Dogs of this breed were ideal for such flights due to their small size and even temperaments. Being a stray was an added bonus, because Laika was strong and able to endure hardships.

'No one knew Laika's history so I presumed it was similar to mine. She was probably a stray not through choice, but owing to circumstances. My nomadic existence was by contrast the result of my own making. I left home and country in my early twenties, wishing to go beyond the confines, prejudices and habits that surrounded me, to break free from the existing boundaries. What made me run away was not so much fear of settling down, but of settling down permanently into something that could eventually turn ugly. I travelled far and wide, discovering that even though each world had its own validity, the only reliable centre was to be found within me. Today, looking back, I still don't know whether it was strength or weakness to have rejected a more "secure" life, but at least with the existence I chose, there was a permanent conflict which kept me alert.

'There came a time when the urge to settle and raise a family got the better of me. One cannot tell for sure, but I would like to believe that Laika had also tasted the awesomeness of motherhood. For me it was slightly different, since it was not simply a decision for procreation but also a choice of the most aesthetically satisfying form of suicide: marriage and forty-eight hours crammed into a day. In order to experience this moment of heavenly creation bringing children into the world, one had to go through a great deal of external submission. Herein lies as much: the habitual force of beauty and the beast.

'Like the bitch, I gave all I had to equip my offspring as best as I could, knowing full well that they belonged to the world, not to me, and that time would come when we would have to step outside our framed existence. If I am to be honest, I must confess that it was very hard to learn how to let go, to give space, to be. My only comfort then was the knowledge that love was not a chain, but a guiding light for all. The future was theirs, but for me the earth I inhabited had turned into a great temple deserted by the gods. All my idols of years past now had feet carved out of clay instead of ancient stone. So I decided to launch myself into space, distancing my life from this Earth's gravity. Like Laika, I had to travel light, leaving behind all I had possessed and known. But carrying oneself is not a light matter.

'As with most historical events, details of what happened to Sputnik's mission have only recently been revealed. Temperatures at the launching space at Tyura-Tam were below zero and Laika was put inside the satellite not on November 3rd but four days before. Electrodes were attached to her body to monitor her respiration and heartbeat. She was fitted with a special harness and a dispenser to supply food and water in gelatinised form. The Soviets knew at the time that they had the means to launch a satellite, but they did not have the technology for a successful load return back to Earth. Laika was the only animal knowingly sent into space to die in the name of progress.

'In the early hours of that freezing morning during the launch, Laika's feelings and mine were similar: frightened and apprehensive of what lay ahead. Pulse rate went up by a factor of three, and at peak acceleration the respiration rate increased four times over pre-launch values. As we recovered from the initial shock, we floated into weightlessness. In the metallic cell without space and gravity, there was neither innocence nor liberty. Surrounded by an immense emptiness, discarded from life because it had left no imprint in our memory, we witnessed the struggle between light and dark. Carrying images of the Earth, the mountains and the faithful fleeting sea with its waves reaching the shore one by one, and then setting off again for the unknown, we orbited. I thought at the time that if I were to die far away from all that was familiar, at my final moment the sea would flood into my cell and help me rise, above myself.

'Seen from a distance, the world seemed beautiful and serene. It possessed a coherence and harmony not apparent in reality, as one failed to see from afar the details of corrosion present in people's lives. I wondered if this was beauty's secret. Rejecting reality and extolling only certain selected aspects, or trying to give form and unity to an impulse that permanently shifts and changes, like a river.

'During the fourth orbit Sputnik got unbearably hot and Laika's breathing shortened. I took her harness off and held her next to me. Clinging to her, I kept telling her that she had to live because I wanted our love to last, even if it was incomplete. "I am the beast," I told her; "Frighten death away." Laika's big brown eyes stared at me as if to say that, were I human, no doubt I would do as you say, but a poor beast that wants to prove its love can do nothing other than lie down and die. Resting her head on my heart, she slipped away, challenging the world anew and bringing closer that day when God might finally stare at us with a perfectly white clear glance.

'At that moment, a roar split Sputnik's metal frame through the deep silence, and the beast within me reared up. As light fell on Earth, it illuminated its wrinkles and wounds, revealing the tragedy of our era for the first time — a world subordinated to production that has ceased to be creative. My whole existence suddenly was shaken by one thought – I must return to Earth. I need to touch Mother Earth once more, even if it is a place of crucifixion.

'Inside Sputnik, Laika's lying machine, darkness descended. Drifting in the chillness of my own shadow, in the absolute stillness, suddenly my memory recalled a wild flurry of notes pouring out of Charlie Parker's saxophone. In this far-away region surrounded by frozen fragments of matter left over from the making of our solar system, music became my salvation, excess to moderation. As I orbited round and round waiting for gravity to suck me in, music gave form to all and everything I loved upon this Earth.

'I had been out in space for thousands of days and travelled millions of kilometres. Taking my hand-mirror, I looked at myself. Through the dark water of the glass reflecting the elusive wholeness of a fractured self, I saw the claw marks of age. By now all I longed for was timeworn smells built up over time, old clothes and books, and old lives waiting to be consumed in time. Fatigue eventually attacks everything, even metal, and Sputnik, tired of orbiting, finally entered into the Earth's atmosphere and burst into flames.

'It is at that precise moment of explosion, when life reaches such a high temperature, and blood and soul mingle together, that one learns to live at ease with contradiction and accept that, if one single living thing had a definite form, we would be reconciled. I realised that beauty alone could not start revolutions but hoped that a day might come when revolutions would need beauty.'

III.

Hermes was surprised to find out that humans were travelling in space. He only knew of Icarus' flight, which had failed dismally. Either a lot of progress had taken place or humans had been ostracised in space due to hubris, as was the case with Asclepius for daring to revive the dead.

Thinking a visit to a city might be the appropriate next move, Hermes tightened his winged sandals and took off. Cities were stretching out everywhere, wrapped in grey-yellow clouds. Hermes had never seen anything like it before. He was not sure what city to choose, so he asked Hestia's advice, she being the goddess of domestic life, home and hearth. Hestia told Hermes that he could visit any city and any house because, even though they looked the same, each one always told a different story.

'I arrive home tired, and what do you do? Draw and paint all day long, then complain because I am late. If at least you wanted to exhibit your art, I could understand it. But you don't. You hide it in the loft. People at work keep on asking me whether we are going to have any children. What do I say? My wife is against procreation.'

His words sunk inside her like frozen fragments of matter. But Miranda, staring intensely at her husband, replied as if she heard nothing.

'Did you know Zoroaster and Hesiod were inventors of the myth about time and age we are all trapped in? According to Hesiod, there are four successive ages, each lasting a thousand years. The first is of gold, the next of silver, then comes bronze and finally iron. Each one represents a decline on the previous one, apart from an unnamed period interspersed between bronze and iron. This is known as the age of heroes. Sometimes I feel I belong in this era.'

Leaving him staring at a switched-off television, Miranda went to the bathroom. She always escaped there as if it were an intensive care unit where one was allowed to display intense grief. Opening the taps, she listened to the noise of running water; as it whirled in a perfect circular motion, she closed the plughole. She sat in the bathtub and poured in lavender oil. Behind the door, her new blue silk dress hung on top of a white cotton towel. It was a present from her husband, whose name was Achilles Papas.

Steam travelled high up on the baked earth tiles, fogging a rectangular mirror and easing the creases in the new silk dress. Slowly, as reality around her was siphoned away, Miranda sunk into a dream-state, transporting her back...

She was a ten-year-old. Her parents had moved into a new house where pets were not allowed and she was forced to give away her cat and dog. Her grandparents, who lived in a detached house with a big garden, offered to look after the dog while the cat went to friends in the country. Even though she would go and see her beloved animals as often as possible, little Miranda desperately missed their presence. However attractive and stylish the new house seemed to everyone, for her it felt like an expensive mausoleum.

One evening as she was having her usual stroll with the housekeeper, Maria, Miranda heard a chorus of plaintive mewing. Dragging Maria by the hand, she followed the sound and after a few minutes discovered three abandoned black kittens by the side of a yard used for storing old building material. Without a second thought, Miranda decided to take the kittens home. Maria protested, fearing her mistress's reaction at the sight of the uninvited creatures, but there was no point trying to reason or go against Miranda's impulsiveness. Miranda knew full well that, regardless of the fuss she made, Maria would eventually take her side. She relied on the fact that Maria's loyalty rested with her rather than her mother, the imposing Artemis Amelia Mitropoulos.

'You cannot side with any human being of inferior breed or social status to yours. It is not befitting,' Artemis always reminded her daughter. Defining and firmly adhering to such boundaries was Artemis's mission. Frequently Maria would burst into tears when reprimanded and, until her eyes dried, Artemis would show compassion. Then with the swift ease of an experienced trapeze artist, she would flip back into her chosen posture of power and control.

Maria's life story was not uncommon, but to Miranda, whose experience at ten was confined to the world around her parents and school, it seemed tragic. Maria's mother had died when she was nine and, being the eldest of seven children, she had been expected to find a job and to leave home. In those days, being poor gave one the right to push young girls out of the house in pursuit of a better life, and becoming a domestic in the city was considered a fortunate opportunity. As in some dystopic fairy tale, Maria had been ejected not into the lap of a prince, but into that of Artemis Amelia Mitropoulos. It happened during a weekend excursion when the Mitropoulos family stopped for a drink in the derelict coffee place of Maria's forgotten village.

When it came to cleanliness Artemis Mitropoulos always touched the borderline of hypochondria. Whenever they went for a meal to a restaurant or even a coffee place, she would venture straight into the kitchen before the owner understood what was going on. Swift as a swallow, Artemis would move from saucepan to saucepan lifting lids, smelling food, inspecting the clothes, hair and washing facilities of the staff, all this in seconds. No one could sit down until she had emerged from her expedition nodding and lowering her eyelids to signal that one could safely eat.

It was in the bowels of this remote Greek village while trying to locate the second most important locale of inspection that Artemis set eyes on Maria the first time. Artemis's large nostrils could normally detect a familiar smell leading to primitive versions of Thomas Crapper's invention; however, on this occasion they failed. That's when Maria had appeared carrying two heavy buckets of water, a quick improvisation for flushing a cistern.

'Does Madam need to visit the throne?' asked Maria. 'I am just bringing water so you can wash your hands. The government has been promising for years to bring us running water but have done nothing yet. Who knows, we may be lucky in the next election. You look like city people. It must be a blessing not to have cisterns, wells, and buckets.'

Artemis had liked the face and attitude of the girl. Perhaps it was her straightforwardness, perhaps a recognition that she was different. Whatever the impression or incentive, fate also played a part; and when Maria's father pleaded, 'Take her, take her with you, she may be only seventeen but she is a good girl, she can clean and cook,' Artemis accepted – they could always do with an extra pair of hands.

Thus, thanks to a lack of running water, Maria's life had changed irrevocably, and she was siphoned away into the Mitropoulos world. In no time, she learned to say thank you and please, her large brown eyes dilating into saucers when Artemis explained how things were done in their bourgeois household. Maria was required always to wear a blue dress, a white-laced apron and bonnet, apart from on Saturdays when she could go out. Eventually she got to grips with the stifling, boring daily chores and a happier atmosphere prevailed between employer and apprentice. However, Maria always ate alone in the kitchen and never joined the rest of the family during meal times.

'The servants place is in the kitchen. If you encourage them too much they will climb all over you,' was Artemis' stereotyped answer to Miranda's queries about sharing and the schism between haves and have-nots.

It was true that Maria's table manners were not of the best. She chewed like a grinding machine with her mouth wide open, out of which pieces of matter flew like missiles, hitting whatever or whoever happened to be in proximity. When Miranda tried to make a point that people ate with their mouths shut, Maria gave a look of disbelief.

'Why'?

'Because you can blind people.'

'How'?

'Because food can hit them straight in the eye.'

'I never heard of people blinded because someone was eating with their mouth open.'

Teaching table manners to someone who had starved much of her life proved somewhat problematic, but eventually Maria learned to chew properly, wash more frequently, dress up and look pretty. She did not mind not sitting at the table with the Mitropoulos family anymore, because she was fast becoming a city girl, living in a modern brave world.

Was it the sight of the three abandoned, starving kittens that reminded Maria of the life she had left behind? Was it awareness of her upward mobility? One could not say for sure but, whatever the reason, she ended up carrying two of the kittens back home. Maria gave them milk, and Miranda put them in her doll's unused pram and covered them with a pink cotton blanket.

Artemis returned home slightly later and, after making sure that the household's daily routine was in order, sat in the lounge reading a book. Maria had cleaned, cooked, polished the silver and taken Artemis's only daughter for her normal stroll before an evening meal. A third member of the family, Artemis's husband Jason, was absent, working late as usual. Everything appeared the same as ever as darkness silenced another ordinary day; but then, in the middle of the night, the kittens woke up, all three of them mewing in different pitches, their plaintive cry spreading through the stillness of the house.

Jason and Artemis Mitropoulos woke up and set out trying to locate the source of the disturbing sound. Finally they entered Miranda's bedroom. There was a lot of furore and shouting at the discovery of living matter inside the basket, but fortunately the uproar was diffused because everyone was still half-asleep. In the morning, George, the family's driver, took the kittens to the vet to dispose of them in the way he thought best. Artemis, upset at being forced to commit such an inhumane act, was comparing herself to a Nazi and, naturally, blaming Maria for her failure to control Miranda's irrational actions. Holding her protruding Cleopatra-like nose next to Miranda's face, she laid down the law in a sombre and assertive voice: from now on, any four legged beast that could walk or create a sound would never again cross the Mitropoulos's front door.

Turning off the taps, Miranda sank into the lavender foam, soap flakes wrapping her body in a delicate cocoon... Not long after the cats incident she had brought home a rectangular green paper box one afternoon after school. Rushing into her bedroom, she had hidden it among her books in the bookcase opposite her bed. The bookcase was stuck in a corner of her room next to the balcony door and concealed from general view. Inside the box were nine silkworm eggs. Miranda had seen them for the first time during a natural history lesson and had become besotted.

'The Bombyx mori was cultivated for centuries in China, its native country, but now it is domesticated and no longer known in its wild state,' the teacher had explained. It was the words 'domesticated' and 'wild' which had rung a chord deep in Miranda's soul and, at the end of the lesson, she pleaded with her teacher to let her take the silkworms home and look after them. Her teacher had hesitated but then accepted the offer, relieved at offloading an added responsibility. He told Miranda that the larvae would hatch in ten days' time and she had to find the leaves of a white Mulberry tree, since this was what they fed on. Miranda had nodded affirmatively but had no clue what the tree looked like or where she could locate one.

Three days went by, and she was unable to discover a white Mulberry tree. The solution came from Maria, who discovered the box while dusting the bookcase. At first there was a shriek, then hurried footsteps to the balcony where Miranda was sitting, drying her hair in the sun.

'What are these things in your bookcase? Where on earth did you pick up these small, unusual goat turds?'

'They are not Turks, they are Bombyx mori,' replied Miranda with a knowledgeable expression half hidden behind her fall of black hair.

'I don't care if they are ex-bombs or whatever, what are they doing here, and what will Mrs Artemis say when she finds out about your new discovery?'

'They are silkworms. They stay in their box, don't run and make no sound. There is nothing mother can say. In a few days the larvae will hatch and they need to be fed with mulberry leaves. The problem is, I cannot find the leaves. I wonder whether these wretched trees exist. I keep on asking my friends but nobody seems to know. What can I do?'

'You mean these, these things make silk?'

Miranda nodded and, pulling her hair from her face as if opening a curtain, stared helplessly at Maria.

'There were mulberry trees in my village square. I know what they look like. I saw some down the Avenue, not far from here,' was Maria's unexpected reply.

Artemis could not comprehend why Maria had decided to

take her daughter for a walk on a Saturday, but she accepted the offer, taking the opportunity to surprise her husband and visit him at work.

It was harvest-time, a warm autumn afternoon, when the two of them started off in sweet pursuit of the mulberry trees. After a twenty-minute amble, they saw them stretching in a straight line all along the pavement of the busy roadway. They stared at the trunk, then at the bushy leaves and finally at each other.

'I cannot reach,' was Miranda's desperate statement. 'It is too high.' Gazing at Maria she realised that she was not much taller. The only solution was Artemis who, apart from her formidable looks, was also tall.

'How are you going to persuade her? She will probably take the silkworms to the vet,' Maria replied gloomily.

Miranda was not sure; all she knew was that a child could always find a way to a mother's heart, even if the mother was the unbeatable Artemis Mitropoulos.

'Mother, I know God is deaf.'

'Deaf? What makes you think God is deaf?'

'I have been praying for so many years to have a brother or a sister and nothing happens. If God could hear me, he would understand how lonely it is to be without a brother or a sister. God does not help me and you have forbidden me to have any animals to keep me company. A dog's life is better than mine.'

Guilt like the malevolent biblical serpent enwrapped Artemis. Giving birth had been a horrendous and painful experience, and she had vowed never to have another child, even though she had felt let down for failing to produce the expected heir and secure perpetuation of the Mitropoulos name. Every time she was tempted, usually when one of her friends had a new baby, she had kept on reminding herself of the ordeal and persuading herself that, after all, it was not her fault. She had fulfilled society's expectations as a woman and wife. The provision of adequate Y's was Jason's responsibility. It was hard enough having to cope with Miranda's moods, sulking and demands.

'My darling, it is not that I don't want you to have pets. We cannot have them in this house. It is part of the contract.'

'Why did we have to move in this house? They have taken my dog and my cat. You never think of me, do you?'

'Of course I do. I always think of you. Don't you like your big lovely room with a double bed and a balcony? How many children your age have a double bed?'

'I don't like the double bed. It is too big and cold, and I never asked for it. You did not know what to do with it when you decided to buy single beds for you and daddy, so you gave it to me.'

'But when your friends come and stay you have such fun sleeping on the same bed. You say so yourself.'

'When do I have friends staying with me? Once a year?'

'Oh come on, Miranda, you are being unreasonable; and for heaven's sake stop sulking. You should be grateful for all that you have.'

'All I want is my pets and I cannot have them. I want to go and live with grandma.'

'You know you cannot do this, because of your school.'

'I hate school.'

'Your school is the most expensive in the country. You should consider yourself privileged being part of such an advanced educational system.'

Miranda knew she had to escape the trappings of adult reasoning and concentrate on feelings.

'I don't think you love me, you wouldn't care if I dropped dead.'

'How can you say such a thing? Of course I love you and care; you know that.'

'Because you say so? Grandma says that love is not a word. She says we have to show love by doing good.'

'But my whole life is an action of love towards you.'

'No, it's not. I am not allowed to have my animals.'

'What do you want me to do? Either we have a beautiful big house, or a zoo.'

'What if we have animals that don't bark and have no four legs, and don't run and create problems?'

'What kind of animal is this? Prehistoric or unborn?'

'No, they are Bombyx mori.'

Artemis Mitropoulos was by no means uneducated but she could not figure out what this animal was that her daughter was talking about and why she had said 'they'. For a fleeting moment, she wondered if Miranda was under psychological strain due to the move and parting from her pets and all she needed was motherly reassurance. Artemis felt nervous at committing herself to something she did not know, but not wanting to lose face and wishing to appease the child and get some peace, she said in a low furry voice:

'Darling, if your animal does not have four legs, and does not make any noise or create any disturbance and is small and insignificant, I am sure you can have one. No one will notice, and it won't be a breach of contract. Are you happy now? What did you say your animal was?'

'Bombyx mori, silkworms. I have nine silkworms.'

Miranda watched Artemis' pupils dilate, but she knew that winning the first stage in a battle did not mean one's objective had been achieved. Timing was of the utmost essence in these dealings if one were to progress further. Hugging her mother's curved yet stiff body, Miranda spilled out a request for the silkworm's dietary supplement before Artemis had time to digest the image of nine worms crawling through her household.

Artemis sat in the chair supporting her immaculate face with her right hand. How could she pick leaves from trees in the middle of the Avenue? Most of her friends passed there daily. What would she say if they saw her? Perhaps she should go at night when no one was around. Why couldn't Miranda be like the daughters of her friends? Why did she always have to ask for the most difficult things?

Miranda, rubbing her self on her mother like a small kitten, confirmed Artemis unspoken words.

'Thank you, Mummy; I knew you would help. Grandma says that if you do something good, you can become lighter, like a feather.'

Artemis never went to pick the mulberry leaves. She sent George instead. Ten days went by and the larvae hatched. Nine white furry little worms, curving and stretching like minuscule silent accordions, started chewing away at the leaves which, after the feast, looked like misshapen pieces of green lace. Never before had the Mitropoulos household been so engrossed in a non-anthropoid manifestation of life, including Jason, whose busy schedule left him hardly any time for family. He too joined in the daily inspection of the Bombyx mori, puffing his pipe as he bent over the box in order to have a closer look.

Each silkworm doubled in size thanks to the mulberry leaves and after six weeks started spinning its cocoon, a continuous silk fibre up to 3000 feet long. Miranda watched them slowly disappear inside their silk houses. There they would pupate for two weeks, hidden from all eyes, including hers. This period was the most important for them and for Miranda. She had to make up her mind whether to let them go through nature's full cycle or burn them in the oven to prevent the silk from tearing. The thought of burning them alive was repulsive: scenes from her parent's tales about the Holocaust kept appearing in front of her eyes, like a horror movie. If she sacrificed one, how could she choose which one out of nine? It was an impossible dilemma, so she decided to let them all go through the stage of metamorphosis. She loved the magical meaning of that word. It reminded her of the frog who transformed into a prince.

Miranda watched the cocoons for long periods hoping to pick up a sign showing presence of life. Nothing. Just a ball of silk wrapped in silence, as if the air was pumped out of the worms' existence... She tried to imagine how it felt being enclosed in a cocoon by pulling her bedclothes over her head until she could breathe no longer. She even took one of Artemis silk scarves and covered her face, hoping to experience a metamorphosis. But nothing happened.

It was an ordinary morning after it had been raining all night – the kind of soft, monotonous, misty rain that often fell at that time of year, washing away summer memories burned on hot sand. The piercing and unfriendly sound of an alarm made Miranda jump out of bed, her heart beating like a muffled African drum. She went to the window and pulled back the curtains. Outside the city's landscape was emerging in faint morning light. Yawning, she slipped on a dressing gown and went to look at the silkworms. Holding her cheeks with both hands as if they were going to drop, she gasped. In front of her a miracle had taken place, making her lose the balance and unity of the world she had experienced up 'til then. The cocoons were torn and nine big white butterflies, a, kind she had never seen before, were glued in place, like fateful stains clinging to the earth. She stood immobile watching this new life, trying to store up the miracle in this ordinary grey day. She wanted to yell, but could not.

She wanted to cry, but could not. All she could do was sit there and watch, knowing that every moment counted. The butterflies had only two days of life left.

That day she refused to go to school. No sweet talk, no threat, nothing in the whole world could shift her away from the moths. In exasperation Artemis asked Jason to interfere.

Miranda's father went to her room and sat next to her, his pipe clutched between his teeth. Jason was a quiet, thinking man, who spoke little. With time, Miranda had learned to appreciate the moments of silence between them.

Inhaling deeply, he closed his eyes momentarily. He then tapped his pipe, emptied some black ash and, pulling a knotted piece of tobacco from a leather pouch, stuffed it in the round hole, pressing it down with his index finger.

'A transformation with such humility,' he said pensively, gazing at the silkworms. Stretching his hand, he touched with a finger the wing of a butterfly. He touched it with such tenderness that it seemed as if it must be the wing of an invisible angel. It was then that Miranda noticed that her father's wedding ring was missing. She felt a sharp pain inside, but said nothing. Instead she burst into tears.

'What is the matter dear Miranda? Why are you crying?'

'Because it is unfair. All this waiting for a miracle to happen and then they have to die so quickly.'

'A miracle cannot go on for long, my child, and with a new life also a new death follows,' said Jason in a low voice and, giving Miranda a long hug, he added: 'Remember this experience of metamorphosis and remember that I love you.'

The silkworms lived one more day, then died as silently as they had arrived. Miranda experienced a metamorphosis too. Her cocooned existence was torn when her father left home and her parents split up, during the year of the silkworms. But now a knock on the door and her husband's voice brought her back from these travels into the past.

'What on earth are you doing in there? Are you all right? You have been in the bathroom for nearly an hour.'

'Have I? Yeah, I'm fine. I was day-dreaming, thinking, about my paintings. Perhaps I should have an exhibition, expose myself to the world,' she mumbled.

The water in the tub was getting cool. Miranda dried herself, glancing into the misty mirror, and then looked at the blue silk dress. She combed her hair, sprayed on some perfume and came out of the bathroom.

Achilles was sitting in the lounge watching television. Crossing the hallway on tiptoe, she went quietly into the bedroom and switched on a light. Her gaze rested briefly on two small, identical, wooden frames hanging on the wall. Behind the glass, nine silkworm moths were pinned on a blue background. Switching off the light, she lit a candle and went to bed wearing her blue silk evening dress.

Watching the flickering candle flame, she drifted slowly into a bottomless well of memories until sleep, like a butterfly's wings pinned on a child's back, carried her into the silent world of dreams.

IV.

Hermes liked the metamorphosis of the silkworms and hoped the story would not create problems with Zeus, who was the master of metamorphoses. Hermes had once been asked by Lamia to help her get rid of her serpent form so she could pursue young Lysius, but unfortunately the transformation had failed. Perhaps metamorphosis was a way of escaping the absurdity of daily existence, thought Hermes. Wondering whether the failure of family unity was due to climatic conditions or the extinction of fire in the hearth, he decided to visit another household.

Flying out again, he reached a city by the sea. He thought if Poseidon ever came back he would not dive into its waters. They were grey-blue, and strange bits and pieces floated on the surface. Tall buildings sprung up all around, and people rushed in and out of them holding to their ears strange square boxes they were talking into. Most of them looked like they were talking to themselves. From high up, they gave an impression of moving like a nervous colony of ants. Hermes decided to visit a building that looked relatively new, hoping Hestia was right.

On an old ferryboat modified to a small passenger liner like so many one sees island-hopping in the Mediterranean, Iris was crammed in a congested lounge with numerous others seeking refuge from a stormy sea. As the boat tilted from side to side, chairs and tables kept swinging, along with the passengers. The room was like a dance hall where inanimate objects and people frantically waltzed to an indiscriminate blend of screams and bangs. Suddenly the captain's voice surged above the pandemonium loud as thunder.

'Someone has to go out on deck.'

Iris stared at a man squeezed between her and the deck door. He was young with dark eyes and curly hair, detached and unperturbed by the motion and panic surrounding everyone. Feeling her gaze penetrating into him, he turned his head and looked straight in her eyes; then something really weird happened. She felt that she had metamorphosed into the young man while also remaining her actual self. Without understanding how it transpired, she realized that the door opened and both of them had been pushed out on deck.

A huge wave and wind gust threw her to the floor against

her husband Phaedon. He was alone, crouching, oblivious of the hell around him. With one hand he held onto a thick metal rod and with the other clutched a folder to his chest. The waves with merciless rhythmical accuracy kept concealing and revealing his large body.

Iris looked around to locate the young man, but he was gone. Taking a notebook out of her pocket, she handed it to her husband. Miraculously, the moment she did this, the sea quieted, turning instantly into a summer day's calm.

'Can you look at this page? I would be grateful if you could correct it.'

Snatching the notebook impatiently, Phaedon scribbled something and handed the notebook back without uttering a single word, as if she hardly existed. Over the years Iris had learned that there was little point in asking him for help. He always resented it and complained of how hard-pushed he was while she indulged in a life of luxury, making her regret that she had dared to ask him in the first place. Despite this, there she was showing him a piece of paper not even knowing what she had written on it.

Suddenly, without warning, a huge wave swept the deck snatching Phaedon and throwing him overboard. Iris rushed to the side of the boat. A thick white rope stretched from the surface of the sea towards its dark invisible bottom. Phaedon was holding the rope pushing himself downwards instead of upwards while behind him the young man was following him towards the depths of the sea.

Climbing on the rail of the boat, Iris swung out ready to jump into the water, but then she realised it would be impossible to save them. She could never hold her breath long enough; they had gone too far down.

Perched on the rail she yelled: 'Men overboard' with all her might, feeling futility, despair and overbearing sorrow coursing through her like lightning.

The scream was so piercing that it could have cracked the bowels of the boat. Only there was no sound, as if the voice had exploded like a silent supernova inside her. The agony and helplessness of centuries seemed enclosed in this soundless scream reverberating through her, penetrating every neurone. Then suddenly, the boat started to turn, as if her mind had given it an order. As it slowed, she felt that Death had touched her shoulder with his bony hand.

Perched on the rail, she looked down. The rope was still stretched into a sparkling clear sea but now she could see lying at the bottom a body shrouded in a white sheet tied with ropes like an Egyptian mummy. Phaedon was firmly holding onto the rope, pushing his body nearer to the shroud, but the young man was nowhere to be seen.

Iris tried to get up, but could not. She lay in bed paralysed, immobile, listening to her own breathing as if she were stretched out on a plank of wood between earth and sky, having aged hundreds of years in her sleep.

'It is a dream, it is only a dream,' she kept telling herself, feeling her heart pumping blood into her lungs with big bellow-like contractions. She had awakened at the critical moment of a fatal turning point. Had she remained in the dream for another second she probably would have lost herself forever. She tried to move her limbs, but it was no good: they were frozen. She tried to scream but her mouth and tongue did not move. She was filled with hopeless terror, one she had never experienced. Something inside her where existence had lodged all these years had died, leaving a vacuum. With great effort she opened her eyes. Phaedon was asleep next to her, his mouth half opened, snoring like a train entering Paddington Station. She thought that perhaps she was in a trance, but she was not. The familiarity of the bedroom made her fear slowly ease, and her limbs started moving again, first the toes, then the legs, finally the hands. But her scream, that scream in her dream, never found a voice. It was still locked inside her like a polyphonic silence broken by the explosive blast of a shotgun.

She switched on the lamp by her bedside. Her husband's sleeping head moved and a groan interrupted the fearful climax of a snore. His nostrils twitched. Through the dim light of the room, she looked at his face trying to remember when it was young. She could only recall its expression from photographs. The face of the man sleeping next to her for twenty odd years looked tired, worn, stubborn, covered with a fleeting expression of arrogance mixed with childish innocence. She pulled up the bedclothes to cover him and switched off the light.

Unable to sleep, she got out of bed and went to the children's room. They were sleeping like angels that still had time left before entering man's treacherous world.

Taking a glass of wine and some chocolate from the kitchen, she went to her office, a large room at the top of the house. Sitting at her desk, she stared at the white wall. This was her retreat. At night when everyone was asleep, she would go there and sit for hours staring at the wall. Sometimes she would write, sometimes she would read, but mostly she would do nothing but absorb the perfect stillness around her, emptying herself into the white plaster.

She kept thinking about her dream. She knew it had to do with survival coupled with loss. Dreams were not simply safety valves for her; they always previewed signs of things to come. The difficulty was being able to understand their meaning because there were never words, nothing spoken, only powerful feelings unlike those experienced in daily life. Iris wondered whether her dream was connected with her health and a recent brain scan.

She had not been well for a while. For three years she had had terrible dizzy spells losing her balance completely and walking like a drunkard. She had said nothing for a long time, thinking they would eventually go away, until one night the children woke her up because a friend who was staying over with them was feeling unwell.

Iris had been alone with four young children, Phaedon being abroad as usual. She had tried to get out of bed but lost her balance and, as the ceiling spun round, fell on the floor. Fortunately she did not hit her head, but fear of being unconscious with young children on her own made her call a doctor in the morning. The neurologist was surprised at the clarity with which she described her symptoms. He said it could be a virus or, worst case, a tumour on the brain. Iris took this calmly and went the next day to have a Pet Scan, concealing the doctor's suspicions so as not to upset anyone.

At the hospital she could not come to terms with the thought of entering the long white tube. She was claustrophobic and told the doctors she would die from asphyxiation. They were understanding and reassured her that they would be speaking to her all the time and that she could watch them through a little mirror in front of her eyes.

Breathing deeply she slid inside the sparkling tube, stared at the mirror and concentrated her thoughts on the doctors' faces. They talked to her non-stop from behind a glass partition. She had no idea how she managed to stay for half an hour without panicking, but she had no other option. She knew she was changing, but no one else seemed to notice it.

Lighting a cigarette, she looked at a chart the neurologist put in front of her. He told her to keep a daily diary of everything she did. She read it back to herself carefully.

'Woke up had coffee, the children had breakfast, took them

to school, came back, cleaned, put on the washing machine, drove to the supermarket, planned the evening meal, grabbed a piece of bread and cheese. Phaedon came home for lunch, then went to his office again down the road. Continued with household chores, stole some time and played the guitar, did some research for an interview. Got in the car to pick up the children from school. Had a chat with them about their day, fixed dinner, helped with their homework. Phaedon dropped in, had coffee, saw the kids and went back to the office. The children had a bath and watched television. We had a chat about their day and I put them to bed. They wanted a bedtime story so I improvised one. Phaedon came home for dinner; we ate and watched the news. He went back to the office. I put things away and soaked in the bath. Phaedon returned; we watched a bit more of television, went to bed, had sex. He fell asleep. I got up and went up to the office. I stared at the wall and scribbled some thoughts. Had a glass of wine and smoked five cigarettes.'

Iris read the diary as if there was no connection between that woman and herself. There were two of them: the one in the diary performing day after day like a car with its engine revving permanently, and another with a mind floating in a different sphere of reality. Perhaps the problem was not necessarily a tumour on the brain but a cancerous life where the protagonist could not find a way out. How could she not lose her balance? It was her body crying out for help. Her daily life was not expanding. It was trapped in a cul-de-sac, proceeding towards an icy execution of not being.

Iris's eyes sank into the wallpaper. Tomorrow she would know the results of the scan. She might be fine, she might have three months to live, she might be about to die and, if so, was there something she would have missed out?

A short stiffening ran through her spine as if thousands of

ants had entered her bloodstream. What was death? No one knew. Perhaps it was a perfectly pure act. If it were a long sleep, it would be fine; if some energy remained or we moved to a parallel universe, it would also be fine, If there were nothing, that was fine too. What was the fear for then? Perhaps missing out on life? Iris lit another cigarette and thought of another dream she had had a long time before.

In between earth and sky there had been another world, a world like a thin slice of earth floating in the space between. Iris was meeting someone important in a cemetery but did not know who he was. It was a glorious sunny day on this slither of the world she had entered and, as she opened the cemetery gate, she saw a dark-skinned woman in a bright red dress dancing passionately and with incredible vigour on top of a grave. It was strange for such a turbulent expression of life and flesh to be present in a place where death was the keeper. The woman danced as if a pulse of fever were springing out of earth's numbness.

Standing there looking at her, smiling with a joy that absorbed language and thought, Iris nearly forgot that she had an important appointment. She had no idea where she was going or with whom she was meant to meet; all she knew was that she had to be there and somehow things would fall into place. Which is what happened. After wandering for a time among the tombstones, she found a grave she knew belonged to her Greek grandfather. On its right corner, a man was sitting, his dark curling hair bending to his chest.

'I knew I would find you,' Iris exclaimed cheerfully.

The man lifted his head and to her amazement he had no face. It was white and blank like a sheet of paper. Yet she knew him without knowing him and she also knew he was there because he could give her an answer.

'What is the meaning of life?' Iris asked him.

He replied with no words.

'Was it as simple as that? But I always knew it.'

In vain Iris tried to figure out the answer when she woke up. She could not because the faceless man had never spoken. What she knew was that she understood something fundamental and simple but did not know what it was. For years she had tried to decipher the riddle inside the enigma, to no avail. She had finally accepted that the dream had to do with life's untold essence, which perhaps she was now betraying. Her only salvation was to follow come what may her path through the mist and clouds of uncertainty.

Stamping out her cigarette, she mumbled, 'This too must go' and went to her children's bedroom. They were still sound asleep, believing the world they had known would be the same forever, though it was about to change radically. Gently stroking their curly hair she kissed them and quietly closed the door... the door to a way of life she was going to leave behind forever.

A few weeks later she had another dream, about flying. She had been obsessive from the age of three about her ability to fly. She had tried to climb over her family's house balcony and take off, and it was only due to her mother's athletic constitution that she was saved. Seeing her child climbing over the rail, her mother had leapt like a tigress and caught her mid-air. On another occasion Iris had climbed onto her grandparents' kitchen table, stretched her arms and landed on the ceramic tiles of the floor, bruising herself to her grandparents' distress. The adults' explanation that humans could not fly was in vain. Iris insisted they could. Finally, when she was around six, Iris's father took her on an airplane journey, thinking it might ease the problem. She was so thrilled that it was nearly impossible to get her to disembark when the plane landed.

It was not strange that Iris from her earliest years had recurrent dreams of flying. These continued even when she had begun flying all over the world in adult life. She dreamed of flying over nocturnal cities until, at some point, gravity would start to pull her down and she would crash to the ground. Over the years the times she could remain in the sky without falling got longer, but eventually she would always crash. This dream kept coming on and off until her mid thirties. There was always frustration at the end when she could not continue the flight. But her recent dream was totally different to the ones that had gone on before.

She was in a large hall. The whole structure was of translucent white marble and the room immersed in light. As one entered, on the left a teacher was standing surrounded by a group of children listening to him speak. On the right was a beautiful winding staircase leading to somewhere undefined. The staircase reminded one of the Renaissance period. Iris had entered without being noticed. The teacher was talking about paintings and art, but there were no paintings to be seen, just the marble walls and tall windows reflecting sunlight. As he was describing an invisible painting and the colours in it, the teacher stopped as if in a trance trying to recollect the artist's name. Iris, who had been silently watching and listening, answered from the back 'El Greco' and started to climb the staircase. The teacher thanked her.

When she had reached the top of the stairs, she opened a wooden door that led out to a veranda. It was a completely antithetical site to the room below. The veranda was narrow, built with sandstone coloured bricks; it had a low red brick wall all around it and a metal railing resting on top.

It was day instead of night, the time when all the previous flying dreams had taken place. Iris stretched her hands and, climbing on the railing, jumped off and started to fly.

It was the most exhilarating sensation, of utter freedom. She could fly like a super-woman lowering herself but not touching the ground or being pulled by gravity. The feeling was outright liberating. She went on and on seeing the world from high up, diving down and taking off up again, filled with elation.

Iris was still looping in the skies when she suddenly noticed on the veranda a young boy with golden hair climbing onto the railing and, lifting his arms, jumping over. She flew straight towards him, wondering if she could reach him in time and whether she might suddenly be pulled down by gravity. Stretching her arms she caught him mid-air before he crashed on the ground.

She set him gently down to safety and told him never ever to do this again. Iris then took off again flying through the sky and eventually landed, not pulled down by gravity, but through her own free will.

After this dream, Iris never again dreamed of flying.

V.

Hermes was dumbfounded by the flying story. He was the bearer of dreams, but humans seemed to have them too. He wondered whether Iris, the beautiful goddess of the rainbow with multi-coloured wings, had previously visited this household. It might have happened since she had been the swift-footed messenger of the gods before him. As he departed, a most beautiful rainbow was filling the skies, illuminating the grey city of steel.

Hermes tightened his winged sandals and, leaving the city behind for now, ventured towards some large mountainous rocks, though not as high as Mount Olympus. On top of these rocks sat some strange buildings he had never seen before. He came a bit closer to get a better look and saw an old man and a young woman sitting underneath a plane tree. The old man was telling the young woman a story and Hermes, being invisible and at the same time curious, sat next to them to listen.

'It was like taking the flag of life for a sheet to wind up death,' Nefeli's father recounted, his gaze pinned into the misty map of memories.

'It was 1941 during the Italian occupation, just before the German invasion. I was stationed at the naval base on the island of Lemnos, used as a temporary stopover for convoys sailing from the Black Sea. Our unit consisted of forty-nine reserve officers and a commander. Our means of defence was our youthful spirit, forty-nine Mauser rifles, 1905 model, and two Saint-Etienne machine guns, dating from the First World War.

'Having fought hard against one invader, we were now confronting the German forces attacking us from the Bulgarian front in the North and the Aegean in the South, trying to cut through the Metaxa Line. Eventually the frontier in Thessaloniki fell to the Germans and the Nestos brigade, defending it, was forced to withdraw to Mount Athos, in the peninsula of Halkidiki.

'Our unit, being located close to Halkidiki, was ordered to pick up soldiers from the front and save them from capture. We were to sail from Lemnos at dusk – at daytime we were continuously bombed – and ferry them through the night to the base and from there to the nearby island of Mytelene.

'For two nights on the 16th and 17th of April, we ferried the soldiers fifty-sixty at a time, packed like sardines in boats provided by the local fishermen.

'During our last sortie, we had anchored at the small port of Dafni near Mount Athos, the boat packed to the brim with the remaining exhausted men. As we were about to start the engine, the colonel in charge told us we had to delay our departure because he had one more task. A sergeant, another officer and myself were to accompany him.

'Leaving the boat, we started off, not knowing where we were going or what we were supposed to do.

'The colonel was in his forties, slender, with a stature hardened by the demands of his profession. He had an appealing face with restless dark brown eyes, permanently intent, as if his mind were focused on something outside the ordinary reach. I thought he was a man of great sensitivity and culture, yet someone who gave the impression of being unable to communicate feelings or affection, as if his life had been void of such experience.

'Walking through rough terrain on a narrow winding path, we were lost in deep thought, all of us reluctant to break the confining silence that encircled us. Suddenly, as if coming out of the trance of his impenetrable universe, the colonel turned towards us and spoke:

'"I have to deliver this to the monastery," and opening his tunic he revealed a long square parcel strapped to his chest.

'Walking side by side, our uniformed silhouettes resembled figures in a shadow puppet show. All around was darkness, obscuring roots and black stones; the path ahead seemed to lead towards infinity. Our sole contact with the world seemed to be the noise of waves reaching us from the sea below, their giant breathing, and the sweet smell of fig trees. As the winding track became steeper and our footsteps heavier, our eyes focused on the horizon, and the fragmented shadow of a tall structure slowly emerged.

'"It is the monastery of Idyra," murmured the colonel. "We have arrived."

'The isolated building seemed void of life. On its high walls hardly visible small windows and a main wooden gate were firmly shut.

'The colonel looked at us, then knocked. No one answered. He knocked again. After a while, a window opened high up to reveal the dark outline of a monk framed against an ink-jet background.

'"Who is it?"

'The colonel gave his name and rank, adding that he had come to deposit the Greek flag.

'"Please wait," replied the monk and vanished like a ghost.

'We waited in front of the closed door, staring anxiously at the sky fearing the appearance of threatening dawn. It seemed as if an aeon had gone by when the noise of a sliding bolt made us stand to attention. Stamping out the cigarettes we had been chain-smoking, we looked at each other.

'Through the slit of the heavy gate, the ebony silhouettes of two monks appeared and, as the gap widened, what I saw made my life turn inside out.

'In the monastery's courtyard, to the right and the left, aligned monks with heads bent towards their chests were holding candles that flickered like stars on the verge of exploding. At the centre, the detached figure of a bishop glittered in liturgical vestments, a long white beard spreading like a blanket over his ascetic heart. The yard had been transformed into a candlelit cross.

'Leaving us behind, the colonel walked slowly towards the bishop and, kneeling in front of him, deposited the folded flag. He then kissed the cross and walked backwards to the gate, wrapped in the hazy smoke of frankincense. Not a single word was uttered by anyone; no one had moved, apart from us. Getting a last glimpse before heaven's gates shut, I was left like a wondering Byzantine chronicler having lost all sense of time and history.

'Sombre and silent, retracing our footsteps to the port, we

were almost running downhill when the colonel stopped and told us to go on; he would catch up with us.

'We thought he probably needed to empty his bladder and our physical presence was rather hindering. He had experienced danger, death and hardship, while we, having embarked only recently into the journey of bloodshed, were novices in the art of war. Our senses were still unquenched youthful torches of desire. We believed that a battle could be won with a reed and a flute. What ignorance!

'As nocturnal light straddled the hazy horizon, the land's contour stretching towards the sea was still not visible. Having covered quite a long distance, we knew that the port was not far. The colonel was still nowhere to be seen.

'We were getting quite concerned about what to do. Where was he? Should we wait or keep going? Should one of us go back and look for him? The boat had to leave before dawn or it would jeopardise the safety of the men still waiting for our return. Unable to make up our minds, we stopped for a few minutes when suddenly the noise of a gunshot slit the stillness in the air, disturbing the encircling universe.

'We looked at each other in disbelief. Under the lightless, starless, granite sky, the colonel had shot himself.

'Face pressed against the cracked earth, dreams banished, movement arrested, his mission completed,' said Nefeli's father, his eyes full of tears, sliding like drops of dew on a face eroded by the passing of time.

This was the second time in her life Nefeli had seen her father weep. The only other time had been long before, when his mother had died.

VI.

Hermes at first thought that bloodthirsty Ares would be delighted with the story, being the god of war and guts. However once it had reached its conclusion, he wondered whether Athena or even Prometheus might identify with it more. He wondered too if these monks were a new pantheon that had replaced the older gods. Whatever the truth, he was grateful at just being the messenger. One thing was certain: people were still fighting and having wars.

Hermes lifted himself higher up in the skies and saw big metallic machines crossing. They made a lot of noise, scaring the birds and expelling from their tails a cloudy ether-like substance. They moved very fast, and he wondered if he could overtake them. He asked Hephaestus if he would be interested in them and indeed he was. Hephaestus told Hermes that he had been watching the metallic flying birds for years: they carried people from all parts of the world in-side of them. Hermes decided to follow one.

Lands and places re-visited after years were like a mirror in which Urania could see the reflection of her own growth; she could be a visitor visiting herself. Strapping on her seat belt while sucking a sweet, she waited for the plane to take off. The familiar roar of a revving engine slit the silent skies, and the metal bird followed a planned course to its destination.

The modern flying Icarus was transporting her thirty-five years later back to a town where she had spent a year as a seven year old. One of her cherished demoted poets had ended his life there long before her birth. As a child, she had known nothing about him, but she got to know his poetry later on in life and it had left an unfaded stamp upon her. Opening a notebook, she started to write, erasing, reading and writing...

'Shed all hope, you who enter...'
Dante, *Canto III*

Ancient ghosts, tearfully howling over multiple deaths, peer at him as he walks slowly into the sea. The moon's iron light, spreading from the water over an ashen landscape, reflects on his submerging head. His body vanishes under an indifferent crest of a wave into a salty reservoir of tears. A loud thundering pierces his ears awakening him from a deep sleep. He strains to see the bottom but it is too dark and obscure, like the world of a blind man. His lungs depleted of air force him to surface to replenish them. Another breath of life, another exhausted trial to end life's journey and enter the circle of the infinite abyss...

For hours he struggles to drown but to no avail. Waves, having playfully broken their rhythmical movement, wash him onto the beach. He arrives at his house at the break of dawn. He prepares the same breakfast as he always does, but time's motion seems different. It shrinks like marmalade spread on the bread and stretches further than the contours of a broken eggshell. Does he feel fear? No, not really since no one can harm him anymore.

He puts on a suit, folds a tie around his neck and, covering his large head with a hat, glimpses himself in a mirror. A child's wrinkled smile reveals a mixture of wisdom and anticipation, the brown eyes accentuating a dimple on his chin, portrait captured. Leaving the house keys behind, he steps out in to a scorching summer's midday sun. Breathing less deeply than usual, he walks to a shop not far away from the Village Square. A gun is a gun is a gun is a gun...

He is not after poetic licence anymore. All he wants is something tangible that works. Size, form, colour – they are irrelevant. Carrying his lethal acquisition, he walks out of the shop with a sensation of contentment. This rare feeling of self-satisfaction is quickly obscured by familiar shadows of doubt. What if it doesn't work? What if his luck lets him down like last night?

He pulls the trigger, pointing towards a wall. Click. Nothing happens.

'I knew it,' he whispers. 'Thank God I gave it a try. I thought guns were reliable.'

Back at the shop he is told that the gun was not cocked. 'This is a very reliable gun,' says the shopkeeper. 'They fire them at the start of horse races.'

Relaxed and reassured, the poet walks towards his usual coffee place next to the beach, 'The Heavenly Garden'. Was it a coincidence or a subconscious thought that the owner chose this name in contrast to everything the town represented – a gloomy, poor, forgotten northern place, where most surely God must have died?

The poet looks at his watch: two o'clock. He sits down, orders coffee, paper and a pen. Opening a box of cigarettes, (he never smoked) he chain smokes as he starts writing a letter. 'It is time to reveal my secret. My biggest sin was…'

Without looking, he fumbles the packet for another cigarette but it is empty. He looks at his watch again: five o' clock. He scribbles a few more lines. 'P.S.: I advise those who can swim not to attempt suicide in this manner. The whole night, for nearly ten hours, I was beating myself against the waves. I swallowed plenty of water, but every so often, without understanding how, my mouth surfaced for a gasp of air. No doubt at some point, when I have the opportunity, I will write about the impressions of a drowning man!'

He folds the paper, puts it in his pocket, pays his bill and slowly walks towards the beach.

Sitting under a eucalyptus tree, he stares at the sea. The crickets' monotonous, deafening sound beats on his eardrums. Their painful song rises to the heavens as they shed their skin, reaching their short-lived transfiguration.

Witnessed by molten, luminous shadows, the poet's life is nearing zero point. Under a crimson summer sun, he places his left hand on his heart grasping the gun with his right. Everything is executed with meticulous attention.

A bang scaring birds away silences the crickets momentarily. A simultaneous flash follows, like a camera recording an image of limbs, loves and lives before entrusting them to eternity. A small red gap in the grey suit leads via a spiraling tunnel towards an invisible bright light.

The poet is dead, shot through the heart of a borrowed body. A final, ironic, slightly arched smile on his mouth seals the immortality of his tortured words.

Around him, the crickets song reaches a frenzied peak.

The stewardess rolling the food tray asks Urania if she is a vegan. 'I am afraid I am omnivorous,' Urania replies smiling. 'It has to do with survival.'

A concoction of food wrapped in cling film is placed in front of her. She picks at the bread and cheese and drinks a small bottle of red wine. Not only omnivorous but selective too, she thinks, and closing her eyes she recollects...

For a brief period her father's career had diverged into politics and he was appointed prefect in this godforsaken place. They arrived in midwinter; snow was covering the ground and surrounding mountains. Their house, even though it was the best in town, had no central heating, only a coal stove and fireplace. There was not even a proper bathroom; one had to warm water in buckets, then sit in a zinc tub and throw the water with a saucepan. She hated the evening bath because she always felt cold. In vain her mother tried to turn misery into fun. The poverty and melancholy spreading round the place was its most striking characteristic. People were sombre, their backs bent as they walked, appearing through the mist like unexpected phantoms or empty-eyed dying prisoners. Youth was swept away from the children's faces, leaving them looking like cloudy shreds of dawn.

It was in this town that Urania saw the masks of death, of utter poverty and of deprived lives, for the first time.

At the local one-room school she attended, life was not easy either. She was singled out, rarely spoken to, and disliked by other children, who saw her as an alien. Philipos, one of her classmates, was older than her and the leader. Scruffy, unwashed, he was one of seven offspring of a mother struck down with tuberculosis, as Urania found out later. Philipos was always fighting with everyone, unruly and impertinent, with an inward energy. Urania was able to forgive these apparent sins, apart from one: his habit of throwing stones at birds with a sling and killing them. This was unacceptable to her and one day, plucking up courage, she went over to him during a class break.

'You have no right to kill birds. They are meant to fly and not being brought down by your lethal stones. They have done nothing to you and they cannot fend for themselves. Why do you do it?'

'For fun. There is nothing else to do.'

'How can you kill for fun?'

The boy shrugged his shoulders, his lips pouting twisted into a knot and he lowered the eyes.

Looking at him carefully, Urania realised he was barefoot and there was snow on the ground.

'Why are you walking barefoot in the snow?'

'Because I have no shoes,' he replied and walked away.

Urania could not understand how it was possible not to have even a pair of shoes. When she returned home, she told her mother that she disliked going to school and did not want to return. Her mother tried to figure out what the problem was, to no avail. Finally Urania said:

'I am not going to school unless the children have shoes.'

'What do you mean?' her mother asked perplexed.

Urania told her what had happened that day. Her mother made arrangements immediately the next morning, providing shoes and ensuring that kids would not walk barefoot on the snow anymore. Urania went back to her one-and-all-embracing cold classroom, and there her first friendship was born, between a boy and a girl.

Philipos knew more about death and poverty, Urania about protected life here and there. This was perhaps their initial bond. They did not know yet about love that moves the stars, the sun and the moon. There was closeness between them, and at the same time a distance, which bound them like an invisible golden string. Their diametrically different backgrounds mattered to Philipos, but not the way Urania behaved. For Urania, what mattered was Philipos's honesty and the way he shared whatever he had or knew, however uninspiring or unfamiliar.

On another sombre afternoon in the deflowered provincial little town, they were sitting on a high wall, their feet dangling, rhythmically moving forward into nothingness, then knocking back against the bricks, while watching the few people who passed by.

'Look at this town,' Philipos said. 'It is so grey. I like grey colour.'

'I like blue,' Urania replied, 'like the sky and the sea.'

'The sky can turn grey; so does the sea.'

'It does sometimes, not always.'

Suddenly a chant reached their ears, a mixture of lament and Byzantine melodies. Urania stopped, dumbfounded, her feet anchored to the wall.

A procession of people dressed in black like wingless crows were following an open plywood casket. Inside, eyes shut, mouth wide, its crevice stuffed with cotton wool, was the corpse of a man. Hands folded on chest, he seemed to Urania like an old man, even though the skin was smooth. As the procession drew nearer, she was able to look more closely. She had never encountered a funeral procession or seen a dead person. What hit her was the colour of his face – grey-green. Urania had been told that when people die they went to heaven and became angels. The angels she had seen in photographs were beautiful, with skin white and translucent as porcelain.

'Why is this man grey-green?' Asked Urania.

'Perhaps he was ill,' replied Philipos.

'Why is his mouth wide-open?'

'Perhaps he wanted to say something but never managed.'

'Did he have children?'

'I don't know, perhaps not. I don't see any children by the casket.'

'Why do they parade him uncovered?'

'So that people get a last glimpse of who he was. If they shut him in a box, how would they know who is in the box? They have to see him.'

'But he is not nice to look at. He is grey-green.'

'Dead people can have different colours. Some faces are yellow, some are blue, some are grey-green or simply grey. Death wears many masks and visits us all the time.'

'How can death visit us when we are alive?'

'He can because there are many deaths apart from what we know as the final one.'

'Why do you say *he*? It may be that death is a *she* and she is a beautiful girl.'

'Maybe, but I doubt it.'

'What colour is the mask of the final death, then?'

'Red.'

'How do you know?'

'I think it must be so.'

'No, final death wears a white mask.'

'And how do you, know?'

'I do,' said Urania bursting into tears.

'Why are you crying?' asked Philipos, totally at a loss, 'since you did not know the man or who he was.'

'I did,' replied Urania. 'I saw the colours of the different masks.'

'Fasten your seatbelts.' The announcement lifted Urania out of a world of memories as the plane was about to land. A sudden twinge of suspense and anticipation gripped her heart. 'I wonder what it will be like now,' she thought and, strapping the seat belt around her waist, waited.

VII.

Hermes enjoyed flying in company; it was a new experience. He thought Penia, the goddess of poverty, would understand the story better than most and so he called upon her to see the place. Penia commented that it would be fair if good men had the wealth and poverty fell to the evil. She advised Hermes to travel further away from the known boundaries, following the larger and bigger iron birds.

Hermes liked the idea and thought that it might be destiny and tragedy that had given humans the gift to invent things like flying birds, even though it may all have started with Icarus's doomed flight. He tied his winged sandals yet again and started off towards the unknown. He crossed tall mountains snowed under and wondered if other gods had ever settled there, since no one was visible at their tops. He crossed many seas until the flying machine landed on a large island. This too had many large and smaller towns full of houses all looking similar. It rained a lot and Hermes was grateful for the winged round helmet Zeus had given him. He decided to land in a place where lots of these running boxes he had seen were stacked together with no one inside.

She was known as the old tramp who lived in a car. For years now, her house was an old Ford resting on four burst tyres. The car top covered with bits of plastic and strings, a 'do it yourself' insulation, looked like a parcel wrapped in rags. On the driver's door on a faded blue-grey background one read: 'I have harmed no one. I have paid my car insurance and the MOT. I will pick bluebells for you to show you that I'm true to you.'

Every morning the old lady walked down to the health centre and had a wash. Her kitchen consisted of a blackened saucepan on top of a gas camping primer installed at the bottom of a car park near a railway bridge. Winter or summer, she cooked magic potions consisting of bits and pieces of various herbs and vegetables, with some protein thrown in. Sometimes she would talk to herself or sing or simply throw abuse to the wind. She fed the pigeons every day with breadcrumbs and talked to cats. Thalia had seen her pacing the streets in foot-clothes made of rags and newspapers. Whenever their paths crossed, she would smile and say good morning. The tramp lady always smiled to return the greeting, but hardly ever said good morning.

She never accepted gifts from people and turned abusive if anyone tried to give her anything. Apparently she came from a well-off family and was a musician and singer. A breaking point in her life had come when she fell in love. It was during the Second World War and her fiancé had to join the army to fight for God and Country. When the war was over, nothing was the same. He never returned, having been killed in action, and the lady's career stopped dead at that point. Ever after she had lived in her stationary car, wheeling through existence in her imagination, her daily shuffling interrupted only by bouts of singing or occasional lashings-out at an invisible *agent provocateur* who happened to incarnate as an irrelevant passer-by.

One spring morning the old lady's singing, notes too high for everyday humans to attain, reached Thalia's ears. As she cut her way in an oppressed midday drowse through the car park, she found herself following the song half awake, as she was still making her passage into the world of day. The tramp lady was cooking a meal and, as Thalia approached, she saw anemones and tomatoes planted in pots placed around the concrete surface. It was an oasis in the desert of stationary cars, whose owners were confined in offices of the buzzing city, trapped like insects with stretched antennae and shredded wings in a glittering spider's nest.

The old lady and Thalia started to chat. The old lady explained that people had thrown flowers into their dustbins that were still alive, so she had picked them out and repotted them. She had to carry water in a bucket every day from the health centre to water them. Thalia remarked how well the flowers were doing and how surprised she was to see them surviving in the middle of a parking lot.

The old lady asked: 'What is your name?'

'Thalia.' She added, 'I feel the world is beautiful because you took these discarded flowers and vegetables and planted and revived them. I'm sure your singing makes them grow... And what is your name?'

'Miss Smith,' came the reply. 'Do you have a garden?'

'Yes, I do.'

'Well, bring me a bag and I will give you the tomato plants. They are doing so well but they need to be moved, otherwise they will wither.'

Thalia re-potted the tomatoes Miss Smith gave her. They ripened red, firm and juicy, like children of the sun. The best tomatoes she had ever tasted, they had grown out of freedom and poverty, by choice.

In return for the tomatoes, Thalia gave the old lady a box of chocolates, which to the amazement of the neighbours she accepted smiling.

In the course of time Thalia moved away from the neighbourhood and her life changed, as did the old lady's. Years afterwards she asked her daughter, who still lived in the area, what happened to the old lady tramp. To jog her daughter's memory, Thalia recounted the lady's life story as she knew it or thought she did.

Thalia's daughter was surprised at the story her mother told and thought it a figment of her imagination. She had another version, having witnessed the old lady's life till the end. This factual account was quite different.

The old lady's fiancé, if he ever existed, did not die in the war, and heartbreak over him was not the cause of her living in a car. She had been thrown out of the family house by her relatives. They had lied to her, maintaining that they were going to refurbish the place, and once she had moved out they sold it without informing her. Her car was parked all those years in the street opposite where her home had been.

The old lady was not a singer, even though she sang beautifully, but a pianist and her name probably was not Smith. In fact, her name was not mentioned at all. The end of her life was also connected with wheels but this time moving ones. It was during a period of unexpected torrential rains that flooded everything. She got run over by a lorry.

It may be that this version of the lady tramp's story was what actually happened, but to Thalia the aura of the life she had witnessed was more powerful, creative, true and humane. She wondered which was more real: a report about a tramp who lived in a car and was run over, or the taste of ripe tomatoes grown in a car park by a lady whose songs travelled over the railway line straight into one's heart?

VIII.

Could freedom ultimately be wrecked by reality? Could fate and chance be the unknown powers? Hermes wondered. Perhaps Mnemosyne, the mother of muses, would identify with this human story and have some answers. Hermes flew a bit higher in the clouds towards the sea and another big city sprang up. He was pondering where to go next when Aphrodite whispered in his ear asking if these humans ever really fell in love and if there was any proof of it.

Hermes wanted to go somewhere quieter than this new city, but Aphrodite insisted and in a coy manner promised him a night to remember in her company upon his return. She said that Eros and Himeros would show him the way. Eros somehow got confused by the traffic signs, noise and furore all around, so Hermes was taken of all places to a sanatorium as it was called. From the outside it looked like any other building encircled by trees and bushes. A freshness was in the air compared to the city's pollution.

After tasting the rigours of life away from her homeland, Sappho returns from her lengthy escape penniless and ill with TB. The only way to survive is to enter a sanatorium, where she can also get food and shelter.

The place is gloomy and smells of oncoming death. Unable to share a ward with others, she asks to be transferred into a small room that looks more like a prison cell for those about to die. Sappho livens the room up by sticking posters of her favourite poets on the wall and a picture of Christ, whom she considers to be another great romantic poet.

She is expecting a visit from the love of her life. They have not seen each other for a number of years as she falsely believed that her lover had deserted her, fluttering off into foreign arms. Pacing up and down in her small room, Sappho talks to herself:

'Eleven o'clock. United by thousands of miles between us, dissecting crucifying us like orphans in desert lands. Ha! They don't know how our spirits fuse.'

Staring at the posters on the wall, she goes on:

'I have reached the end of all endings. Only because you

held me in your arms one night and kissed my mouth, only because of it, am I as beautiful as a blooming lily. Only because you held me, my soul still shivers. Only because you loved me so beautifully was I born. I hide my tears in my palms stroking your face with two rivers. I know the deep story of your every wrinkle. Your eyes penetrate the dark soil of daily uselessness and boredom we both tried to escape from. Too much of it – we were engulfed. To be wrapped in your warmth, only that... I am so hot, burning.'

She opens the window and keeps talking:

'Where does death end and life begin? Where does love rest? On which note in between? Death held my hand the moment your love touched me.

'All is alien. People are all the same. Empty churches, towns where I am a misfit... a captive lion roaring in winter.'

Shivering she shuts the window:

'It's cold and cramped in here. I feel like fire. No, I won't see you in this cell. I need space to float so you won't concentrate on my appearance.'

She looks at the clock on the table.

'Time moves so fast it almost seems static. Ah well, a sunset will catch another sunset.'

She coughs nearly choking and starts again.

'How violent is the wave that surges from my guts taking me up to its crest. Love of my life, I stared into the iris of human eyes too long searching for you. Reduce me to ashes. Like an eclipsed sun. Is there still time? How foolish I am. We are shadows carrying the image of a dream. My dream is wild and wide, stretching in an endless night lasting longer than my life's boundary. Did you recognise the depth of the black pain engulfing me, or did you only rest on the smile spreading on my lips? Did you see me folding myself in your love like a butterfly resting on an untouched flower? I scattered as far as I could love's inebriating song from the depths of my heart so it would reach you gently.'

Sappho stares at the clock again, gets up and looks at herself in a small mirror hanging in the corner of the wall.

'I could walk through aeons. My eyes are as black as night with circles as dark as volcanic ash. How can I conceal it? I don't need pity; it's love I want. I am so pale. Perhaps I will put on a red dress; it would be apt – the colour of love and blood. I can't wear white: I might get buried in it.'

Sappho takes off her black gown and slips her skeletal body into a bright red dress, accentuating her pallor. Still looking at the mirror, she talks on, watching herself as if she was someone else.

'You'll soon be here. It feels so strange being so far away, yet so near. We will sit next to each other and talk of all that has gone by, of everything that has died, before losing it. Of the expectations we failed to fulfil and the decay taking over our lives. Of the dreams, oh yes! the bright dreams we lived momentarily as earth crumbled away. In the stillness of your presence our last words will burn out.'

She sits on the bed and her expression changes from dreamy to alive, nearly aggressive.

'If only I had locked away the treasures of my soul. I threw my life to the four corners of the earth. Life! You were my light, so bright it still covers pain's mania. My voice full of blood reaches your every wound via life's frenzied dark vision. Yes, I was born because you loved me. I must not let you know how your words turned me into a drunkard with a desire for death's bittersweet wine. I feel so hot. My body is on fire and inside I shiver. I hope the reception room will be sunny. All I want is to lose myself in your eyes once more where you hide silently life's bitter secret.

'Did you understand? I wonder. Revenge was not aimed at you. It was all mine. It was the silencing of knives cutting me up. It was revenge against the eternal memory haunting me forever. Because you loved me so beautifully.'

There is a knock at the door and a voice announces that a visitor is waiting for her. Sappho replies she will be out in a moment. She gets up, straightens herself and opens the door. Outside the passage is dimly lit. Walking steadily, she places her hand on her heart as if wanting to stop it from beating, then walks through the narrow corridor erect as a statue.

IX.

It is strange, Hermes thought: when in love, mortals do not metamorphose into something else. They either seem to die of love, or love seems to die. Yet it marks them forever. Perhaps love has a different meaning when one is mortal, replied Hades, who made rare appearances on Earth, preferring to stay in the Underworld, but the call to duty prevailed. 'You should visit a burial place,' he continued. 'In there, love and death co exist, and it is very quiet.'

Hermes flew over another city not dissimilar from the previous one. He mused that up in Olympus things that are seen and things that are not seen harmonise. The gods did not abstract the outside world in preference to the world within. He wondered if it was the same among mortals. Reading his thoughts, the goddess Iaso came to his aid, guiding him towards a tall oblong building with many windows. In a courtyard at its base, people were shuffling around as if waiting for something.

'How can you see?' the eye surgeon asked, perplexed.

'With my mind I suppose,' she answered.

'Why did you not do something about it?' he continued.

'I was told the operation would be unsuccessful, because my eyes could not cope with the brightness of light.'

'If you want to continue in your profession, you should have the operation as soon as possible. Even if it is against the odds.'

'Is there serious risk I might lose my eyesight completely?'

'There is always a risk, but we will deal with the weakest eye first and then, after three months, with the other. Do you need some time to think it over?'

'No, I have no choice; let's go ahead with it. I trust you.'

Hearing the anxiety in her voice, the young doctor shook her hand, adding softly: 'I trust you will be all right. I'll see you in a month's time.'

Theia waited with mixed feelings for the day of the surgical intervention. When it arrived, it was relief on one hand, because finally something would be done, and apprehension on the other, because something could go wrong. Theia recalled talking to the surgeon of the different worlds she saw in her dreams; they reappeared during the operation while she was awake.

She was launched into a great ring of pure and endless light, where all was as calm as it was bright. Floating coloured shapes appeared, leaving behind hues of blue and mauve. Suspended in a timeless zone, travelling through purple and red tunnels, amidst flashes like exploding stars, Theia was lost until a voice surfacing from the guts of the Earth echoed in her ears:

'Well done, blood pressure is OK, wear this patch at night in case you scratch your eye. I will see you in a week.'

Theia had witnessed the new miracle of the twentieth century, the restoration of a photographer's eyesight, performed by a doctor behind a new machine, even though the heavens still remained a mystery.

Clinging on to a nurse, with unsteady steps she left the operating theatre. 'Are you all right?' asked the nurse.

'Fine,' she replied, and entered the light like a heart cleaving to a guillotine's blade.

She was petrified. Trapped between walls, thumping feet, mouths biting empty air and unknown people with scanning eyes, she touched surfaces and groped her way slowly towards an exit, following a smell of freshly brewed coffee. Smell is a strange way of seeing, and at that moment it gave Theia temporary reassurance.

Pushing the hospital door, she ventured out. Her eye was cauterised by brightness, tearing away the prisoner's clothes that had become one with her existence. Mist covering her vision lifted, exposing a frightfully stark world.

Theia felt like a midnight drunkard, having lost his way. All around her silent people walked fast, like burned out coal on the grey pavement. Noise was piercing, as if she had been operated on for deafness. Her breathing accelerated as her eyes in the air fluttered, infected by pollution. In front of her, cars of all shapes, colours and sizes devoured every inch of space. A woman dressed in black was driving a blue car; perhaps she had got married driven in a white car. An older man in a white shirt was driving a red car; perhaps he would be carried away in a black car. Two children, a boy and a girl, were sitting at the back of a grey car; perhaps they were born in a car. Red light, green light, stop, go. Rushing feet, squeaking wheels, indescribable sounds, like bees fleeing from a burning hive, all mingled within the bric-a-brac of suburbia. Ahead, billboards portrayed smiling women and men looking alike. Through the cutting edges of their smiles, a new god of greed was emerging, made from the dust of all the others. How can humanity put up with such an artificial paradise? How could beauty find a place between the gaps of aggressive graffiti sprayed on concrete walls? The world was swimming before her eyes: publicity, consumerism, capitalism, burgeoning population, mass communication, individual isolation and inveterate apathy. Where was the country's green elegance? What was this alien place she had been thrown into?

Like a lost time traveller, Theia stood at the edge of an abyss holding a padlock. Until recently childhood, country, past existence were far away, hidden behind an invisible blind. Now they emerged frame by frame in front of her eyes, as if seen with binoculars through the glass darkly. Panicking, she hailed a cab. All she wanted was to hide in the safe familiar space of her house.

Once there, her breathing became normal. Touching furniture, she moved from room to room. Staring out from the kitchen window, she saw trees stretching above red rooftops. Closing her new eye, she glanced through the old. Everything was misty. She then looked through the new, closing the old. Everything was bright, flooded with light, leaving nothing to the imagination. Which was real: what she saw now or what she had seen before? There were two worlds, the same and yet different. How would she get used to this dichotomy? How would she function? Would she be able to take photographs?

Needing nature's solace, she grabbed her camera, her only faithful companion throughout these years, and walked towards the park, which was only four minutes from where she lived. It was a park she knew well. Or at least she once had known it well. Now that she could see all, she wondered if she would recognise what she thought she had known before. Photographs could be her salvation. The old camera might help her figure out whether she could still capture what was visible, yet invisible, to the naked eye.

Theia walked across a bridge stretching over a pond, photographing squirrels, ducks, flying birds, blooming flowers and the delicately veined leaves of plants. Taking a rest, she lay on a bed of soft-rotted needles, under the shade of a yew. Beneath its canopy, she felt like entering a world of tangible silence. The yew's branches, spreading towards a bright blue sky, looked like human faces and limbs. Were they real, or was it an illusion created by light as it fell on the dark bark? Most trees died of old age, but yews quite spontaneously began an era of new growth that repeated itself for thousands of years, making it impossible to define their age. They were a symbol of everlasting life. Staring at its contorted form stretching towards the light, like a lost soul emerging from the depths of the earth, Theia wondered what age it had reached. She took a photograph without looking. She didn't need to look. Sensing the tree, she felt like the tree; only her roots were aerial.

Leaving the sheltering yew unwillingly, she followed a winding path along rows of statues and imitations of ancient Greek temples and captured their reflections in the water. Further down, locked in a small room behind a black iron gate, she discovered a statue of a Sphinx that she could not remember having seen before. Yet she must have done. Resting the camera between gaps in the gate she took a series of shots. She wondered why this statue was inside a room; was it because people were afraid of the enigma? its mystery? She took a few more shots and, as she turned the camera sideways, she caught through the lens trees reflecting between sky and water. She kept opening and closing the shutter speed, wondering what was she seeking with such despair, photographing shadows and the statue of a sphinx, locked like a silent prisoner behind bars. Perhaps she was suffering from post-operative shock, having been so suddenly exposed to harsh light.

That night she had a strange dream. She was standing upon the Earth, but the Earth was without form. All around her was pitch darkness, as if she had been thrown to the bottom of a well. Slowly she distinguished another human form, covered in a long hooded coat.

'Who are you?' she asked.

'I am Tiresias, the blind Theban prophet.'

'What do you see?'

'I foresee what you see. Vision is not about seeing things. Whatever discoverable exists, lies within.'

'I could not see and yet I could, now that I can, I don't know if I can see. Please help me.'

Tiresias turned slowly towards her and she realised he was just a talking shadow. 'This is a night scope, it will show you what you need to see,' he said and, handing her a glittering object, he disappeared.

She woke up, her heart beating fast. She wondered whether a night scope existed, and why the dream was dark and without colours.

Feeling her way around the furniture, dragging a chair, she reached for the window and pulled the blind. Outside, perched in the sky was a full moon. It was neither yellow nor silver, but more a ring of pure and endless light spreading like a newborn love upon her windowsill.

Sitting by the window, wrapped in night's lesser light, she absorbed its mysteries in total serenity, until slowly and unobtrusively day's greater light covered the skies.

Turning around, Theia glimpsed her room looking bright and pleasant, as if ready to greet an old traveller back home. Walking around pots of plants without touching the furniture, she wondered whether the night scope also included a day scope, to help her cope with daylight.

A few days later when Theia got back the photographs, something very strange happened. It was probably a coincidence, a double exposure.

The sphinx on the photograph rested free on the ground. The walls had vanished. Only the Iron Gate remained, but it was moved into the background, behind the statue, leading towards light and water. On the left of the photograph, above the gate it was night time, on the right it was daytime, while among the green young cypress trees, a lit lamp shone in broad daylight. As for the trees reflecting on the water, what appeared in the photograph was the shadow of a person with both hands lifted up towards the sky as if holding something or on to something, while the feet were resting on the surface of dark blue water. Above the shadow, a tree branch, turned golden by the falling light was bending down towards the shadow.

There is always a logical explanation, and things are as

they are.

But are they as they are? Was the gate in front of the Sphinx or the gate behind the Sphinx? Was the Sphinx inside a room or outside? Was the shadow Theia's or not? How did one know, since it was a shadow? Was the shadow holding a branch, an invisible camera, a night scope, within a day scope, within a life scope? Did it matter?

Well, this was not solely about matter and perhaps, who knew? At evening time it should be light.

X.

Hermes thought the gods would find it interesting that machines were curing people now, and perhaps Asclepios might be allowed to return from his exile. He wondered if people still needed a helping hand from the gods or not. They may have been getting wiser, living in harmony – if so,

Athena certainly would be pleased – or they may have been turning into something else more in tune with their machines. But what, he did not know. Haephestus perhaps might be able to shed some light.

Hermes tied on his winged sandals again and went to the place Hades had suggested. Rain was belting down on and off; people were complaining about landslides and floods. Poseidon too, who very seldom joined the rest of the Olympians, was informing them about volcanic unrest in the depths of the sea. I wonder what the world is coming to, thought Hermes as he followed the next story.

Throwing a shopping list into her battered handbag, Olympia locked the door and left for the supermarket. Glancing at an ominously dark sky, she decided after a moment's hesitation to leave her umbrella behind, hoping her optimism might alter the weatherman's forecast.

Shopping done, she stepped out into grey day with a sigh of relief. She had walked a few yards when the heavens opened. Toting her heavy recycled orange shopping bags, she rushed for cover under the yellow and green tent of a newspaper agency. Having nothing better to do while waiting for the storm to abate, she read the small ads stuck on the window like a scattered jigsaw puzzle. Suddenly her gaze rested on an unusual hand written request.

'Person required to look after two graves twice a month at near by cemetery preferably an old pensioner.'

The thought of two graves uncared for, abandoned under the grey sky like forgotten wandering souls, filled her with a wave of tender sadness. With an impulsive gesture, she took a pen out of her bag and scribbled the phone number on her hand while waiting for clouds to rid their final watery load.

Back in her house, having finished the day's tasks, she

stared at the number absorbed on her skin like a tattoo. There was no name or any other clue to help her make a decision, just a feeling that whoever had written the ad showed respect for the dead and therefore respect for life. The number once belonged to a central London residence. An image came to mind of an elderly housebound widow unable to look after her husband's grave.

Plucking up courage, with a mix of curiosity and anticipation, Olympia dialled the number and waited. A woman with a posh accent answered. Not knowing exactly how to start the conversation, Olympia burst into a flow:

'I saw your advert at the newsagent and I felt sad about the graves. I am a Christian Orthodox but not religious. We take care of the graves and always make sure there are flowers. I am sorry, but I'm not an old pensioner as yet. Have you found someone?'

'No, I haven't,' the woman replied, 'and I was getting quite concerned because I have to leave the country at the end of the month. I asked for a pensioner because I thought they might have more time.'

'I suppose I am a kind of pensioner in that sense. Where are you going to go? You said you were leaving,' Olympia continued in one breath.

'I have built a small house in Greece, in the Peloponnese, and I am retiring there.'

'I don't believe it; such a coincidence. I was born in Greece.'

'Really? It is a coincidence. I could not detect a Greek accent. My father was Greek and my mother English. I never lived in Greece but I decided to move there. The graves are my mother's and a girlfriend's whose husband is buried next to my mother. Unfortunately, my girlfriend died two years ago and, since she had no one over here, I tend her grave too. I am so relieved you called, because it was weighing on my mind what would happen once I moved.

'It is quite extraordinary,' continued the unknown woman who all of a sudden had become like a long lost friend. 'When can we get together? My name is Athena.'

They agreed to meet outside the tube station. Athena said she wore glasses and had white hair; Olympia, failing to give a description of herself, said she would pick her up in a blue car. She arrived at the station at twelve-thirty as agreed. Athena was already there, standing between the jewellery shop and the florist, holding a potted white geranium. Olympia pressed her horn, and Athena's tense facial expression turned in the direction of the sound. Waving out of the window, Olympia tried to catch her attention. At sight of the moving arm, Athena's face lit up as if a veil had dropped away, revealing her identity. Crossing the busy street, she walked briskly to the car. She was tall, svelte, white haired, with sparkling blue eyes behind pale grey glasses' frames and a slightly curved powerful nose, revealing inner strength. In short, she was the portrait of a rare breed of Englishwoman, swiftly vanishing in a fast-changing world.

'You are a sophisticated lady,' Athena remarked, strapping on her seat belt. She had the eye of one accustomed to weighing up men and misfortune.

'Oh no, I am not. I had a meeting this morning, which is why I am wearing a suit. I wear blue jeans most of the time.'

Olympia had had no meeting but, having guessed that Athena was older, coupled with her elaborate accent, she had decided to play it safe and wear a suit.

Battling through heavy traffic like two characters out of an old black and white film, they reached the cemetery's heavy iron gates. It was a glorious sunny day in May. Leaving the car behind, they walked through a sea of crosses and flowers. Around them in the vast field of the dead, silence reigned. Over the high walls that surrounded the cemetery, noises of the city spread like a sibylline murmur.

As they walked along two long rows of identical gravestones, Olympia suddenly halted. On plain, inscribed rectangles set at equal intervals from each other she read the identical date: 1945. Looking at the names and the ages, she realized that all of them belonged to young Englishmen between nineteen and twenty-two years old who had fallen in the line of duty during the Second World War.

Feeling through the prism of time the kinetic energy of firing bullets, she said to Athena: 'These men buried under the stones died so young. We have outlived them.'

'Yes, but our world is never the same after the loss of someone we have loved. We do not get over losses; we merely learn to live with them.'

Olympia, glimpsing the few bunches of dried flowers resting on the graves, mumbled with a low voice for fear of disturbing the quietude: 'I wonder if eternity exists.'

'There is consolation in the fact that the dead once lived and were loved and remembered by those who were alive,' replied Athena. 'Their presence cannot be removed from time. It is a kind of eternity. Who would wish to live forever? Endless existence would be intolerable. The only problem is, one could say, that death may come too soon before our interest in life is exhausted.'

'I am not afraid of dying. Are you Athena?'

'Dying is an act of living; only the living do it. We experience dying for ourselves, as we experience death through the loss of others. Therefore, our own death is not part of our personal experience. Only life, of which dying is part. So, subjectively, one might say we are immortal.'

'Perhaps everything is recycled,' concluded Olympia, looking straight into Athena's clear blue eyes, which reflected the brightness of the sky. Then staring at her shoes, she added: 'When I die I will have only two words inscribed on my gravestone: *she lived*.'

Walking in silence amid the odour of damp flowers, gazing at the slow movement of scattered black silhouettes in the distance, they arrived at Athena's family grave.

'Here we are. There is a watering can behind that bush and a tap over there. I'll go and get it.'

'No, I will, I have to do my job, haven't I?'

Returning with the can full of water, Olympia found Athena on her knees planting the white geranium on her friend's grave. She was a bit surprised that Athena offered it to her friend rather than to her mother, but said nothing. As the water was seeping into the dry ground around the geranium, Olympia looked closely at the engraved name: David Solomon, two dates and at the end 'in loving memory'. She asked Athena why there was no mention of his wife.

'She wanted it this way. I don't think they were married, but they were devoted to each other. They came from Austria during the war. He was an engineer. Apparently his qualifications were not accepted, so they opened a bakery. It was hard work. They lived for each other and had no children. She was a good woman, the type that never complains, submitting out of wisdom rather than weakness. Somehow her life ended after he died. She followed him two years later. She asked me to strew her ashes next to his grave.'

'Where?' asked Olympia, her sternum filling up.

Athena indicated an exact spot to the side of the grave.

'I'll plant a flower there,' Olympia said, thinking silently to herself – a flower which will grow and embrace the whole grave until flower and stone become one.

'Make sure it is not yellow. She did not like yellow flowers.

White and pink would be best.'

Olympia started cleaning the snake-patterned marble surface on Athena's family grave. A big crack running across from top to bottom divided the names of her grandparents from her mother's. Breaking the silence she asked: 'Your father's name is not included. Is he buried in Greece?'

'It is a long story, my dear, and I the cause of the trouble. My mother's parents had a dancing hall. It is a skating ring now. My mother was pretty, a jolly character, she liked having a good time going out with men. In the evenings she used to go dancing and it was during these outings that she met my father. One fateful day a tall handsome Greek entered the dancing room. Their eyes met and I suppose it was what you call mutual fatal attraction; it resulted unfortunately in my mother's pregnancy. One would imagine she should have known better, don't you think?'

'What was the problem, since they were in love? A lot of women did get pregnant before marriage throughout history. Pregnancy is our strength and our weakness. Did they get married?'

'My grandparents were horrified and, since there was no way out, my parents had to get married. If I showed you the wedding photographs, you would understand. Everyone looks miserable. Then I was born and things got worse.'

'Why?'

'You know how Greek men are. They come home at night and expect the wife to cook and generally look after them. Well, my mother was not a domesticated woman. She did not like either to cook or to wait for my father's return. If he went out to have a good time, she wanted to join in the fun.'

'I understand. So did they divorce?'

'After a couple of years my father, who had a fur business, decided to go to America. My mother and I were to follow soon after. We never did. I was brought-up by my grand-parents. I never saw my father again or heard from him. I guess he was embarrassed to contact us after so many years. I was able to trace some of his relatives recently in Greece; they told me he never married again. I don't know. Perhaps they said it not wishing to upset me.'

'And your mother? What happened to her?'

'My mother continued her life in the same way. I did not like any of her boyfriends, but I am more of a sombre personality than her. I loved my mother. She was always affectionate to me,' concluded Athena, removing dead leaves fallen from a rose bush and a jasmine on the grave.

Olympia locked her gaze on the gravestone's lines' always loved and remembered', then on Athena's refined profile. Who would believe it? Two solitary women meeting for the first time, bonding through loss and change, Athena trying to put together the image of the father she had never had and losing her family through changes, Olympia feeling a wave of affection surging up but unable to find a way out. It turned into a commonplace sentence:

'You will be fine in Greece. I know you will. Those who love you will guide you. You can plant vegetables in your garden and have chickens so you can taste fresh eggs again.'

'Oh yes I will, but only hens. And I will get a dog. They don't look after animals well out there. I'm told they poison them, so I will have to build a fence around the house. My friends think it a very irrational decision, moving to another country at seventy-eight. They keep asking me what will happen if I fall over and hit my head? Honestly, I would prefer to go that way than be confined in a hospital bed.'

Handing Olympia a bag with a shovel, some pots and a pair of gardening gloves – the tools of her new trade – Athena murmured, as if at the graves, 'Memories, memories, remembrance of things past is just for the rich. Poor people seldom leave their birthplaces, and their memories are less nourished.'

'What about the heart's memory then, isn't that important?' Olympia asked.

'Of course, they say it is the surest kind, but the heart wears down with fatigue, sorrow and labour.'

'I'll take the watering can back,' said Olympia, leaving Athena to spend a few moments by herself with her loved ones before going away, perhaps forever.

To prolong the time, Olympia decided to walk through gravestones rather than taking the path. Trying to avoid stepping on graves, she hopped among the gaps like a jester who, having given up the frivolities of court, was finally at home with an invisible, undemanding crowd. Suddenly, nearing Athena's family grave, she tripped over a wooden cross that nearly touched the ground. On the dried soil where it half-rested there was not a single flower. As she pulled it back trying to secure it in place, she saw a name written in black letters: 'Esperanza.'

'I think I will have to look after another grave – it is so neglected,' Olympia said to Athena, her face bright as a lake filled with crushed tears. 'The dead woman's name is Esperanza – hope. I feel she would have liked it. Strange as it seems, I find this place full of life and joy.'

'You talked about memories. Is it not strange that the most important lines on a grave are two dates? the day one is born and the day one dies? But I am mesmerised, fascinated, excited, moved, by the unknown gap between the two. I can envisage Esperanza with ebony hair arriving in this country, perhaps from South America to find a better life. Did she find it? Or did she die alone? There are no other names apart from hers. Her name – Hope – though, says it all.'

'I think of her dancing the flamenco or the tango,' added Athena with a smile.

Glancing knowingly at each other lightly, they walked towards the car. They stared once more at the world of flowers, stones, hope, love and nothingness stretching behind them before venturing again into the busy motorway.

Dear Olympia,

I finally settled in my little house. In the evening I watch the most glorious sunsets, sitting in my garden, which looks like a forgotten part of paradise. I haven't got a dog but instead I adopted a stray ginger cat named Tiger. Tiger is very suspicious of everyone but very fond of me. I suppose I will have to take him with me to England whenever I visit. I cannot trust him with anyone. Last night I had a dreadful time. The neighbours next door have animals, and they slaughtered a pig. The noise it was making was horrible. I felt so sorry, and I could not sleep all night. They should have taken it to an abattoir. It could only happen to me, a vegetarian, living next to an animal farm. My other neighbours, in the front of the house, are English. He is a retired plumber, who made lots of money during the house boom in London and decided to come and live here, with his wife. They never smile or say good morning;, they get drunk every night and row. The rest of the people are fine though. When are you coming over to visit me?

Love, Athena

Dear Athena,

I have booked my flight and will see you in three weeks. During my last visit at the cemetery as I was going to pick up the watering can, I saw a man sitting on a posh black grave – you know, the one with the golden letters and the photographs of the elderly couple right behind your family grave. The man was dressed all in black and was talking on his mobile sobbing and looking at the photos.

Do you think he was having a conversation with his parents? It is a weird world, you living in my country where they slaughter pigs in their houses, and I in yours, where people converse with the dead through the internet. I am so happy being a gardener for travelling souls. I never realised, how beautiful ephemeral flowers are and how delicate their fragrance is. It is weird but my plants last much longer than most, perhaps because the forgotten graves hold on to them...

Love, Olympia

XI.

Hermes knew this story might raise some eyebrows on his return to Olympus, since it touched the sensitive point of the never ending flow of people from different regions throughout humanity. Of course all the gods, being who they were, already knew the context of the stories, and up 'til now there had been no anger or displeasure about Hermes's messages.

He was looking for a place where he could relax a bit from flying over this vast, brave new world when Demeter appeared, bitterly complaining:

'You visit places where Hades reigns but fail to report anything about what happened to Persephone,' she burst out.

'But you told me not to reveal the letters exchanged between you and Persephone,' Hermes replied.

'Release them. I will protect you,' was Demeter's answer.

After Persephone's abduction by Hades, Demeter desperately needed some contact with her daughter. She started writing letters to her and asked Hermes to deliver them secretly. During the months of separation Persephone and Demeter were writing to each other while waiting for the time when they would be reunited again. Some letters were kept secret due to the sensitivity of their context, so we are allowed to publish only what they have chosen.

Letter from Demeter to Persephone

My dearest Kore,

I am wandering daily on this forgotten scorched earth without a sense of purpose since you have gone. I have abandoned my responsibilities, all I worked and cared for, searching with Hecate's torch everywhere to locate you. If it was not for bright Helios, who sees everything, to show me what happened, I would have never have found your whereabouts. Child of mine, brightness of my days, now dimmed by the knowledge of your youth and freshness fading in your husband's house, how could you negate the light of life, sharing your tender years with the king of death? How did he trick you? Did you not know this was forever?

It never bothered me that you were born out of wedlock. It was your deceitful marriage, dear daughter, arranged by your father Zeus and Hades, his brother, without your consent or knowledge that made me behave as I did, committing an act against my gentle and caring nature.

How else would I be able to see you? Even if it is for nine months of the year, I had to fight the establishment of two worlds ruled by Zeus and Hades by forbidding and cancelling trade agreements, ruining crops and all kinds of vegetation until the race of men was in danger of extinction. Their cries of hunger pierced Zeus's ears until people's despair and anguish forced him to negotiate with Hades your return. However, again they created a problem. Self-interest, apprehension and diplomacy were unbeatable and your stay is only allowed for a wretched portion of the year. Hermes kindly agreed to forward our letters, but you must be careful not to be found out.

My beloved Kore, I will not use the name your husband uses, 'Persephone', which means bearer of destruction, because you are not; he is. You, who have tasted the food of the dead, the pomegranate seeds, can see both sides of the issue. Both gods were cunning, scheming, selfish and cowardly; Zeus even refused to see me face to face. He had to appease me through a messenger. I try to understand how men think; I even asked Athena to explain it to me, but she only said:' Be diplomatic observant and patient.'

How can you be patient when your child is kidnapped and married without her consent? Of course Zeus, having scattered offspring in so many forms and disguises, worries only when the world order he is ruling is at stake. But I, having given birth to you and carried you for nine months, feel as if part of me has been ripped off together with you.

Men have created war to show off – to pretend they are brave, as if only killing and fear could make one rise to a nobler being. They wish to believe they are powerful. But what is power? And how long does power last? I care about the Earth, about creation and the good for all, how can I understand this schism? or even if I did, how could I want to follow it? All that is left to do is what I did – show to them what it feels like to live in the cold and greyness of winter, when nothing blossoms and nothing sprouts.

Dearest Kore, how can you exist in that sombre place without sun or light, surrounded by shadows all day? you who beat the ears of corn? I warned you that your beauty was also your weakness and that you would be easily tempted by what you desired. As always, mothers and children do not see eye to eye when it comes to that sort of advice – children think they know everything; but such is youth's nature. I only wanted you to rejoice in life, away from the knowledge of darkness – the darkness that such an unsuitable bondage as you are in now can bring. You may think of me as a protective, possessive mother who refuses to let you go to your destiny. Beloved child, it is not so.

For an eternity I have been carrying women's fate, together with Athena. I knew too well the meaning of dark Hades. He'd seduce you and make you dependent. After all, he is king of the dead, dealing only with death. But you, are part of me too. It is I who taught humans how to sow, plant and harvest. I made them learn the rewards of toiling the land. I disguised myself with humility into a mortal woman to be among them, with much effort, persuasion and patience. I wanted the world to be a better place for you. To rest your first glance on the golden fields of wheat blossoming as you turned to light and life on your day of birth. My anger arises because Hades tricked you with the pomegranate seeds I created, with the beauty I had bestowed upon the earth, and acquainted your life with ghostly shadows and darkness.

When your fate was sealed in this manipulative way, I

despaired. I wanted to kill the Earth and all I had created on it. Death reached me too, through you. Forgive me, but my pain was stronger than my love. It is not that I have sought revenge. What revenge can I get when I see the light of my life buried in dark chambers of eerie silence? No revenge could be good enough. I could only make them see how their obscure and destructive powers were less effective than mine. Hades has always been the same. No songs, no hope, no light, no life surrounding him. Where I live, and you did too, among the fields and the people's tired faces, among birth and death, we created a dynamic world full of change. Perhaps your father Zeus wanted to give his brother a bit of all this and, selfishly, looking after his own interest, without consulting with you, promised your life to him.

How then, could I win with the king of gods? I had to play their game. Divine rules are not fixed only for men, but mine were not scheming and calculating. They stemmed from anger and despair at injustice and betrayal. I had to create seasons and mark the earth with consistent changes, keeping winter months to remind them of who they are: gods of oblivion and frivolity, control and power seeking. The rest of the seasons are a reminder of who *we* are, quietly submitting for the good of procreation – more procreation, yet also more darkness.

So, beloved child, autumn is nearing and soon we will be laughing among the old crops of corn laying on the fields until the old and new meet each other again. In the meantime do write to me how your days are filled; about the past lives of the dead and what they are recounting to you. I too will be telling you about how they were before Acheron escorted them to their final destination. Noble souls who go into the depths of the dark Earth down to Hades's house do not die. They become a song to be sung in the future.

Letter from Persephone to Demeter

Dearest Mother,

I feel alone and cold down here with a husband who cannot hope to warm my soul and make me laugh, even if he were to try. I know my duty and I will not complain. I await stoically for the autumn and spring months when I shall happily reunite with you.

The feasts of spring, rejuvenation, rebirth and fertility have no place here; only new death arrivals. Here all that is left of people who once lived, danced, loved, fought, were happy and unhappy, are nothing but pale shadows – shadows that no longer feel nor hope nor love or fear. I, being alive, have no place down here, yet I am bound by bonds of marriage into this world of shadows.

Such a one arrived today. A king of Sparta, the Furies announced. He was a leader of men and lover of women; the commander of a large fleet, a nearchos disposing of ships so large that they could not fit through the straits and navigation ways. So many things have changed over what the mortals call years, yet so many haven't. This new arrival seems to me no different from King Agamemnon who sailed with his magnificent fleet to Troy in pursuit of his brother's beautiful wife and woman.

This nearchos fell in love with a young and pretty girl, but another man of the seas married her, so this nearchos married her sister instead. The two men fought a long and relentless war and, as always, war ends in grief, loss and tragedy. The nearchos possessed riches, victories and glory surpassing any Spartan king. He could inspire selfless devotion as well as boundless envy. He was not an ordinary man, Mother, by any means, but then, those who are self-made kings seldom are. Yet his final prize was the untimely death of loved ones; deceit, hate and resentment followed by sleepless nights of torment and remorse.

This nearchos who has just crossed the Styx and joined us in our gloomy kingdom is now reunited with the shadows of those who loved and hated him during his life. There is no rancour or animosity present here, just shadows wafting noiselessly by, with a flicker of recognition in the hollows where once their eyes rested, admiring beauty.

I wonder, Mother, if you met him while he was on his earthly travels.

Letter from Demeter to Persephone

Dearest Kore,

Yes, I met your new arrival a number of times. Poseidon filled me in with details, some amusing, some tragic the stuff human lives are made of, only on a much larger scale. He had an island, which is why Poseidon knew him, and a very beautiful trireme or yacht, as they call them, according to Cassandra.

He was a man of the land but ended in the seas. Wanted to follow Odysseus's path but, unlike him, never set foot again in his Ithaca. Perhaps it was because he did not have to fend for a Penelope the way Odysseus did. Instead his wife had to ward off the women he would send to his other homes, trophies from trips over seas. Regardless of this, he always remained with his wife and cared for her in his own way.

At least these stories may brighten the dark days at your husband's palace. It may even lift your spirits realising that we gods of the Olympus could not exist without mankind's tragic and comic fate, created mostly by them, not us. We are but the keen observers. It's only those who meddle with human nature and try improving their lot who really suffer

– like Prometheus.

Tell me dearest Kore, how likely is it that you will have any children by your sombre husband? Does he treat you well? Is he faithful to you? You never met anyone else before him; you never had any children and, even though I am deprived from the joys of being a grandmother, I feel relieved that at least you don't have to put up with arguments on whether your children should permanently stay in the Underworld or visit me.

Jealousy, possession and revenge are not solely the prerogatives of mortals but of us too. Your own father and brother of mine, Zeus – was he not angry at my love for the handsome Iasius and responsible for his untimely death? There were of course different conspiracy theories tied up with Iasius's death. Even though one may not know for sure, I think I know the culprit. I wish I had warned you about not accepting food from your captors. If you ate it as you did, you were bound to stay forever with Hades. I thought you knew that. Did you?

Letter from Persephone to Demeter

Dearest Mother,

I don't know about having children – perhaps; who can say? I have to ask Cassandra and will let you know. Yes, he treats me well, but the other day the Naiad nymph Minthe, who was his lover before he met me, dared say that she was superior to me, and Hades said nothing. So I got furious and metamorphosed her into the garden mint. He of course called the plant hedyosmos (sweet smelling). I am thinking of adding it to all his meals; at some point he will get fed up and never utter her name again. The other day he had a surprise for me. He asked me to come down into a cave where he had created a most beautiful garden so that I would not miss the earth so much. He loves me and tries to make me happy; and I too, if I am honest, have started to feel some sympathy towards him.

I took a long walk in the Underworld today and saw three female shadows and one male in between them. Apparently, a young princess had just arrived. She had no direct power but inspired a kind of devotion among her people. She was called the people's princess.

One of the two women was a president's wife. Her husband had been assassinated, and she had been here long before the princess made her appearance. The people's princess also died in an accident and all sorts of conspiracy theories were ripe about both deaths.

The president's widow seemed temporarily animated by the princess's arrival, and especially by her choice of men. The widow could not understand how a princess could surround herself with people so below her rank, who could not protect her properly. How could she agree to go on a cruise on a rented yacht? Why did she not chose a man like she herself had – her second husband after the president's assassination was a real man who ruled the waves and had a yacht with golden taps and stools made from elephants' private parts; a man who could protect her with not one but a whole army of bodyguards, none of whom would flinch from throwing intruding paparazzi into the sea. Her second husband was slightly rough, if one had to be truthful, but he was not a little playboy. This was the way women like them could be taken care of, by choosing the right partner.

I forgot to tell you that the widow's second husband was also a sea-faring king with a huge fleet and an island; he called himself the Alpha and the Omega. He too had been married before, to the girl who was also wanted by the nearchos I've mentioned. It is quite a complicated story but, when you think about what goes on in our own families, it is not so dissimilar. Both men were kings of the seas, but Poseidon did not mind because he knew all this was temporary and would eventually end up with a bang with him not even having to lift his trident.

The people's princess wondered if the president's widow had finally found love and happiness in her second marriage. Guessing her thought, the widow blamed the princess' naivety on the likelihood that she had read a lot of her step-grandmother's books. This step-grandmother was a popular writer of romantic stories. I have no idea what 'romantic stories' means, but I hope she can tell me.

The president's widow's second husband had had a lengthy and much publicized relationship before, to a soprano. The soprano was here too, and she approached the princess in a tender way, because she could understand her despair and need to be loved. Despite her notoriety as a hard and wild woman, the soprano seemed to have the greatest emotions of them all. She was different to them, but then she was an artist blessed with the ability to make one cry and to delight at the wonderful singing she worked so hard to perfect. She accepted that the princess sought happiness in the love of a man, what we call Eros. No one seemed to warn her that the stronger the love the stronger the pain.

Did you know them, Mother? Can you tell me what happened?

Your loving Kore

Letter from Demeter to Persephone

Dearest Kore,

How much I cherished your letter. Its good you have a

garden. Did he plant narcissuses too? the flower you were so keen to smell and wandered away from the nymphs for, enabling him to snatch you? Hades fell in love with you and it is understandable, but what he did is unforgivable. He could have said that he wanted you to be his wife and we could possibly have found a modus vivendi, despite all that had gone before. Violence against one's will is never a solution, and women are there to be cherished not violated.

Yes, of course I knew about the new arrivals in your kingdom of shadows. Kings, queens, princesses – it is like Olympus down there, with a difference: we are immortal, whereas everyone eventually becomes a shadow in the Underworld, Tartare or Erebus.

I knew the soprano. Orpheus used to accompany some of her arias secretly, and the muses would join in when she rehearsed quietly before performing. She was the one who truly loved the Alpha and Omega man. Unfortunately, like Orpheus, she could not avoid temptation. She relinquished her career for him – it was the first time she had been in love, and she gave it all away.

One does not know what he truly felt. After all, she was as famous as he, if not more so. He always wanted to have women who were in the public eye. With all his shine, he was incomplete until they shed their light on him. Omega saw her as another formidable acquisition to add in his collection of trophies. What an irony that the man she loved hated opera and was fond of the blues or rebetika. After conquering her, most likely he got terrified at the prospect of being with a famous woman who had reached the pinnacle of her career on her own strength, the same as he had. So he married the president's widow. What a choice! Many wondered about it at the time, but there were other issues involved, unknown to the public, that made him act the way he did – so Cassandra informed me.

The soprano was heartbroken. He had been the love of her life. They had very good moments but terrible ones too; even Zeus would admit it. When eventually he died, she died too. Locked her self in, occasionally taking a walk with her little dog. A broken, solitary figure, she wilted away, finding no more meaning in life – a life that had been full, successful and rewarding, appreciated by people.

I think at the end he had eventually realised how true her love for him had been. It was her that he saw a week or so after his wedding to the widow, and it was her that he saw on his dying bed when his daughter secretly let her in.

So, child of mine, what can I say about the mystery of love? Those who lived it have gone through pain, and those who have not have perhaps gone through a life void of the untouchable dream. This is what Eros does, and we up here seem trapped in the idealised emotion as much as the rest of mankind. Why do we choose whom we choose? We never know. Aphrodite is the one to consult and, of course, Pallas Athena. Between the two of them lies some faint answer. Yet Aphrodite, attractive as she is, cannot make men fall in love with her, unless she uses her magic girdle or wonder bra – opinion seems to be divided. Everything is a finely cut balance: the girdle versus her lame husband Hephaestus.

I wondered many times if tragedy would have been born if Olympus did not exist, all of us sitting up here watching people's lives and participating on and off in disguise? Is tragedy anything more than the fate followed by a wrong turning on one's path? Like Oedipus, for example. Had he gone the other way, he would not have encountered his father. What made him take the path he did? fate or simply an irrelevant choice? Zeus can interfere in nearly everything, but the only thing he cannot is what the three old women, those agents of destiny the Moirai, have decided. They are the guardians to a universal law of refined equilibrium.

As for the people's princess... she was lucky in a sense, because she died before realising where it could all lead. Cassandra told me at the time what she saw, and it was dire. You can ask her; she remembers better than I, as she is the visionary.

Dear Kore, soon we will meet again, and what happiness that will bring into my life! Make the best of the circumstances, dear child.

Your loving mother, Demeter

Letter from Persephone to Demeter

Dearest Mother,

I met Cassandra today and asked her about the princess, but before answering me she rested her hand on my belly and told me I was carrying a child – a girl. She said most probably it happened when I ate the pomegranate seeds and told me to say nothing to Hades in order to avoid any possible problems and simply wear a larger peplos.

He won't notice it with all these new arrivals. As it is, the child will be born when I am with you, so you will be the first to see it, and she will have her first sight in the light of day rather than in darkness. For nine months she will be surrounded by flowers and sun. Her impressions will be connected with Earth's bounty and colours. I am happy and afraid at the same time, Mother, because it is a new experience and I know nothing about it. What kind of parents are Hades and I going to be? He and I are quite different, I a child of the light and he a man of darkness. I already feel tenderness and protectiveness towards my unborn daughter. Will Hades be a loving father? Will this child make our union better, or will it destroy it? Will he be dissatisfied because it is a girl, not a boy?

I cannot tell you how relieved I am that I will be with you during the birth. In other circumstances I would have liked my husband to be with me, but since he has only the experience of shadows, not real life, his presence might amount to a bolt out of the blue, making him wonder about the grey finality of his kingdom. I hope he does not question the paternity of the child, but since I have done nothing wrong the gods will vouch for it.

This is what Cassandra told me about the young princess. Apparently she went against the interests of earthly Olympus, if I can put it that way. She interfered with the sale of weapons that killed people, and perhaps those interested in profiteering were scared she would go further and interfere with the most profitable global trade: the selling of arms. War is the father of all, and arms means money, lots of it. The princess was treading on a dangerous mine field with humanity, grace and great popularity – a double-edged knife for the powerful ones. She had lovers, that is true, but only because her husband had returned to his old mistress. She did as he did rather than succumbing to the old hypocrisy. Even gods do it, so why not she? As for her choice of the playboy, the last lover who might have been the cause of her untimely death: what was the difference between one playing king and the other playing boy? Isn't that what manhood is all about? Her boyfriend's aunt was married to a renowned arms dealer; this, coupled with the fact that her boyfriend was a Moslem and his father had created havoc in one of the ruling parties, was not good news for her.

When I prodded her about whether she had intended to marry her boyfriend, she declined to answer, saying simply that the outcome of it all was her children losing a mother and his father a son, and the winner being Hades.

I have been wondering, Mother, about Hades. Having spent some time with him since our marriage, I can see that he is not so detached from Earth as one might think, for everything we plant goes under the earth and from there it roots and eventually ripens and blossoms on the surface above. It is dark here, it's true, but if light and sun were on the seeds and roots, they would dry out and not flourish. Of course I love the light and the sun, but for life to keep going it may be necessary for both these extremes to exist.

Do not believe I am having these thoughts because I have eaten the seeds Hades gave me. No, they are solely mine, and, had I lived only in the Underworld or on Earth, I would not have had them. Living in between worlds gives a broader view of the world and its people. So, dear Mother, however difficult it is to be parted, just think that it is only for a while and how richer our lives are as a result of our separate and combined experiences.

Time is nearing, Mother, when we will be together. This is the last letter from me before our meeting.

Your loving Kore

Letter from Demeter to Persephone

My beloved Kore,

What joy and happiness your letter gave me! My Kore is having a child and I will be able to share this experience and become a grandmother.

All my anger and feelings of injustice have momentarily gone and my heart is filled only with elation from this unexpected news. All that matters is your welfare until the arrival of your beloved daughter. Cassandra is right: the best thing to do as things stand is to play it safe and keep Hades out of it until the child is born. One could always say you were not aware of what was going on, since it was the first time and you being so young and away from your mother did not yet know the facts of life. I await your ascent here next month so eagerly! I don't know how I will last until then. I have even thought of tempting Charon with golden coins to take me down the river of woe to your palace so I could see you. But the return trip would have been rather impossible no matter how much I bribed him. Also, having to face your husband's Cerberus dog was a daunting and not particularly friendly or welcoming thought.

Dearest Kore, one becomes familiar as you do with Hades only when one descends in his world. Of course your husband tries to please you and, being wealthy, as he owns all the minerals under the earth, gives you presents and wants you to be happy. A child will fill your lives, yours mostly, and perhaps things will get better as time goes by.

Yes, I knew about the recent visitors to your husband's invisible kingdom. Beware though: appearances even in shadowy forms can fool you. At least your princess fathered her children with her husband – more than can be said of Aphrodite who had all three children by her lover, the impetuous, drunken, quarrelsome god of war, Ares. Adultery, however, cannot be concealed forever. When Hephaestus found out, he told her full of smiles: 'Excuse me dear wife I am taking a short holiday on Lemnos, my favourite island.'

The moment he was out of sight, Aphrodite sent hurriedly for Ares. Hephaestus caught them in the act and summoned the gods to witness his dishonour. It was not a clever move: making their affair public was unnecessary, as your mortal shadows know well. Even Zeus refused to interfere, declaring that Hephaestus was a fool to bring it all out in the open. So, dear Kore, there is indeed little difference between the affairs of immortal monarchs and us.

Is there then, no real love between gods or humans, you may ask. Yes. Athena and Odysseus were the perfect couple. She was deeply impressed by his inventiveness, and he was devoted to her. Their most important attribute was trust of each other. Sadly, Penelope was but the prototype of the faithful wife, a tradition still haunting us. I wonder sometimes whether the true message of her tale was of her faithfulness to Odysseus or her commitment to weaving. Athena was the inspiration, the personification of wisdom, the mediator, the one who made Odysseus's journey worthwhile. The perfect love: between a goddess and a man.

And what about Aphrodite, you may ask me. Beware of Aphrodite. She is canny, manipulative and extremely possessive. She seldom lets go of her prey. Aphrodite is the winner of vanity.

Dearest Kore, I must start getting ready for your coming back to Earth. I will create the most wonderful place for you and your little girl. For a while you will be surrounded by the light of life and your mother's unending love. I may even dare to believe that your husband will venture out more than before, rejoicing in his newborn child.

Your loving mother, Demeter

XII.

Hermes took off, leaving all to chance. This was to be his final journey before returning to Olympus. He saw vast green fields with hills and animals grazing and among them a remote little house with a beautiful garden. He decided to land there. As he approached, he heard a strange noise; Tick Tack Tick Tack Tick Tack. It sounded like a multiple heartbeat spreading around. He was about to enter the house making sure he was invisible when he heard a voice from inside:

'No need for transformation I can guess who you are. The invisible must be understood by the visible.'

As the door opened, an old man with snow white hair appeared, dressed in a long tunic embroidered with butterflies, flowers and bees.

'I rarely have visitors but you seem as old as I am, even though you don't look it. You must therefore be someone from times past. Do come in and make yourself comfortable.

I am Aeon, a horologist and clockmaker – a loner, as you can see, but not because I am fleeing the world of humans, rather because I care too much.'

It was a new experience for Hermes who until now had been an observer roaming over cities incognito and not communicating with people. Aeon, though, was different and so was the interior of his house. The rooms were full of clocks showing different times, all ticking with the dials moving in the opposite direction, from right to left. Some were grandmother clocks, others grandfather clocks, others cuckoo clocks. Others had little doors with silhouettes coming in and out, as if dancing. Further in was a telescope pointing from a window towards the sky. All the walls were covered with shelves full of books.

'Are you an astronomer as well?' asked Hermes

'You could say that I am an observer of celestial phenomena, but I also did construct the chronophagus. It was not particularly noticed or used because people were obsessive about the future, the past and the present as separate entities. My chronophagus does not discriminate, it gulps all.'

'If they are all the same, then how can I exist, coming from the past?' asked Hermes quite bewildered.

'You are a time traveller. We are all time travellers in a sense. Imagining the future is a limiting process. The future is empty and gets filled only by what we can imagine, each one of us. It is a projection of what we are at a particular moment. You can only care about the future; I am part of a life that started long before I remembered it and will continue when no one will know me. The early humans could not imagine the way we are now. Neither could you. You had to visit us to understand what went on from your time to our time. Like recounting a story.'

Hermes understood Aeon's point of view but wanted to

know if there were still any recollection of the Olympian gods. 'Have you ever heard of Kronos?' he asked going further back in time, prior to his own existence, so as to make sure that Aeon knew what went before and after.

'Kronos is *Hronos*, meaning time. I got the inspiration for my machine from him. He ate his children the same way as my chronophagus.'

'Have you ever heard about the Olympian gods and the Olympus mountain?' asked Hermes.

'Of course. Even though so much literature and history perished throughout the centuries in deliberate destructions or during wars, stones, clay and papyrus inscriptions have survived, and the invention of printing eventually saved the life of books. It did not matter anymore whether they were burned or destroyed. At the beginning of course most were stories of people's everyday lives, and religious works.'

'Then our stories remained as well.'

'Yes, because your philosophers and writers wrote about them and were keepers of them. So were your representations and portraits carved on marble and clay by artists at the time. Zeus face is immortalised by Phidias at Olympia as is yours too, with Dionysus.'

'So if something can be saved and stay for long, it can beat time in a way?' Hermes asked.

'Yes, if people safeguard it, since it is up to them to save or destroy cultures. What you call the past is an accumulation of what remains from the wisdom, works of art and all things that humans created surpassing their limitations and aspiring towards excellence; all that has added to the betterment of human existence from the time gods were men and women walking on this earth. Ancient gods though, in principle, leave no place for human tragedy; only human pain and error do. They are steps on the ladder of knowledge. The creation of Olympus was the work of free-spirited people from the ordinary run of life without dogma or fear but an ideal that anyone could pursue in their own different way. It was the best that man could attain, which of course required all one could give.'

'If as you say we were the creation of a time when ideals and needs were different, could the memory of our existence still survive?' asked Hermes.

'All things are full of gods. Everything we do belongs to nature and flows from causes we cannot control, and gods, like travellers from distant zones with different shapes and ways, will always haunt our towns.'

'What do you think then might happen to all of us?' asked a rather concerned Hermes.

'Who knows? Nature will have to follow its course as it has numberless times. Most likely it will be a slow long deterioration, another change. Droughts, floods, crop failures, honey bees gone. Everything is finite.'

'We have seen this already,' added Hermes with excitement. 'It has been snowing without end on Olympus. This is why I came down to visit. To get an idea of what is happening, what kind of lives people are leading nowadays. We have to decide whether to stay where we are, remaining idle as we have been over the centuries, to move further up or to descend and live unknowingly among our people.'

'A lot of changes have happened since your time, Hermes. Machines have taken over to a great extent. Calculations are measured in nanoseconds; technical information is stored in technical clouds, and touching people is becoming remote, nearly virtual. Memory cannot be stored to last, but for a limited period only. What happens when there is no memory of all that has been done? of the effort of creation? Can it last? Or is it ephemeral as if it never existed?'

'You get me worried, Aeon. I came down from Olympus to find answers, and you keep on asking questions. I think I will have to summon Dionysos to brighten things up.'

'Our fates are intertwined,' replied Aeon, laying out wine and bread. 'I wonder if you ever came across Ikaromenippos. He was the reason I bought the telescope.'

'Of course,' replied Hermes. 'He joined us at a do on Mount Olympus and I accompanied him back among the mortals. He went to the moon but his comments about the human race were not particularly favourable.'

'Yes, he was the first astronaut and said that the Earth when looked upon from the moon is a small and fragile surface and that wars and empires appear absurd. He articulated the sentiments every astronaut also voiced during this past century,' replied Aeon.

'He also said that the effort required to gain wealth and power was a hindrance to acquiring things that mattered,' continued Hermes; 'that it was odd that men who had the same beliefs about the same things went to war with each other as gods did. Perhaps I should not have referred to this comment, in case Zeus is displeased. Things, however, seem to have shifted so that pleasing gods may not be the order of the day anymore.' Hermes added: 'After all, we too seem often not to be in unison and not necessarily agreeing about decisions. One thing is certain, though; our lives would be empty without the presence of humans. Empty time was all we could have until they came in.'

'That may be,' confirmed Aeon; 'myths need to be dressed with our flesh to become alive. Yet human affairs seem also to be absurd, trivial and fickle. Being earthbound, how can we have an objective view of any truth? Only freedom of spirit and imagination may show us our individual truth. Perhaps this is a reason we tend to look for answers further away, up in the skies. Today can last hundreds and thousands of years. Your presence and the Olympians' deeds, demonstrate that. Other times it feels like yesterday, for example when meeting old friends from the past. In the future, who knows? Millions of people might be living and working in space. Will this migration be a natural evolutionary process or due to annihilation of all gods except Mars? People here now still think that rocks and crystals are solid when they are made up mostly of spaces in between atoms.

'The world has lost many languages, books, cultures and works of art. Gods too seem to have changed from being revered to being merely admired in statues, icons and stories. I have heard Zeus saying that the Olympians' fate is bound with that of mortals and Athena saying that the owl of wisdom flies only with the gathering dusk.'

'If you were to name something that for the next thousand years might be worth holding onto and communicating, what would it be, Aeon?' Hermes asked.

'Memory,' replied Aeon and, handing Hermes a clock, he whispered: 'Time is ticking...'

Deus Otiosus